The Lunchbox

Jack Croughwell

A Novel

CONTENTS

ACKNOWLEDGMENTS

I would like to thank my mother Rosa, and my father Mike, they are the obvious choices for top billing. Thanks to my illustrious sister Sarah: half for existing and half for the cover design. And a hearty thanks to my editor Patrick Price for smoothing out some literary edges and for humoring me when I badgered him for his secret first name. Thanks also to all children because I find them so gosh-darned amusing. Then, lastly, thanks to Stephanie and Bernadette.

.

CHAPTER ONE

THE BABY BADGER CUB CLUB

It was unlike Nanette to forget her lunch. After spending four years with the firm, she had cobbled together the perfect early morning routine: her first alarm would go off, then the second, the third, and then the real one that got her out of bed and into the shower and through making up her aquiline face. After brushing her pageboy hair to its standard orderliness, she got dressed in the clothes she set out the night before (which in itself was an efficient act because Nanette had a specific suit for every day of the week), grabbed her lunchbox, purse, double checked that she had her keys (which hung from a lanyard around her neck), and if Joey was up and about by then—always a gamble if the kids he worked with wore him out or not—she would wish him a good day. And by a "good" day she would say something like "Do try not to set the house aflame again"—an action Joey had not done since he was seven and Nanette had only learned about it some years later.

Nanette didn't care for the toy trucks strewn about the living room, nor did she like that the countertops always had some apple-scented stain. If it wasn't for her private bathroom she would have to shower at work because, well, the main

1

bathroom didn't have a non-sticky surface. Around six-thirty, on a usual evening, she would roll into the driveway of her split-level house, traipsing up the stairs to the kitchen from the garage, and the last of the parents would be chatting with Joey. They often took their time, as he would fix them a quick snack for the road, perhaps to share with their child. That did not concern Nanette very much. She would walk in, grant a polite hello, and retire to her bedroom if it was a Friday. Any other day of the week she would retire to her office.

Nanette, if nothing else, was a woman of habit.

Which made it all the more strange to her that she would have forgotten her lunch. The question rattled around inside, nearly consuming her morning, because she was vexed by the at-large nature of her lunchbox. Joey, knowing better than to misplace any of his meticulous cousin's possessions after knowing her for his entire life, was more likely to chop off his hand than to mess with a Jansport that wasn't his. So as Nanette pulled up her modest drive in the middle of the work day, eying the plastic candy-colored cars that loitered in the front yard, Joey must have begun to panic in his reserved and methodical ways after hearing a hitch in the routine.

The start of summer was Joey's busiest season. Parents wanting to spend time away from their kids (or parents wanting to spend time with one another, as Joey had frequently explained to Nanette) would leave their children at Joey Abbot's The Baby Badger Cub Club where all the baby badgers come to play. Better known simply as Baby Badger, Joey ran it with his partner, Rich. Both men were new adults at the age of twenty-four. Their housemate-ship began when Joey was twenty-two and she was thirty. Something was mind-bogglingly enterprising about the Abbot name, as Nanette's work afforded them her house in which she allowed Joey's business which, eventually, provide for him a house of his own. However, all this was rather unimportant when Nanette's primary focus lay with an estranged ham sandwich and a side of baby carrots that took up residence in her lunchbox at large.

She pulled into the garage with a mission. Quite some

time ago, Nanette's brain taught her to ignore the overwhelming aromas of Joey's scented candle collection, so prominent a stench it reached to the nether regions of the home. Rather she zeroed in on the mirthful shrieks of the kids using her home as some Hasbro jungle. Nanette hoped none of them had found her lunchbox and decided to use her baby carrots as pretend cigarettes or whatever make-believe nonsense they got into these days. Climbing the darkened steps of a windowless ascension, Nanette emerged in the kitchen, finding Rich (full name Richard Eliot, of the local Eliot fame), who was singing some song under his breath, making a platter full of sandwiches with peanut butter and marshmallow fluff.

Rich was the smallest person of the house. Petite and graceful in appearance, he didn't allow the hazards of working with children compromise the choices he made in dress— which was to say that Rich was still relatively new to working with children.

To her surprise, the kitchen was devoid of children. Their voices emanated in from somewhere in the lower level of the house.

Rich ceased singing when the door shut behind Nanette and the butter knife he held fell onto the counter top with a modest clatter.

"Nanette!" he exclaimed. "Didn't expect to see you in today. You weren't fired, were you?"

"Do not forget to wash that knife before putting it in the dishwasher," Nanette replied. "And no. No such luck. If I was fired, I would not worry about getting back to work on time. My lunch is not with me."

"That's unlike you."

"Yes."

"Did you misplace it?"

Nanette didn't respond. Rather insulted, she just walked over to the refrigerator. Upon opening its door, she found that she didn't find anything. Her lunchbox wasn't there. Just an empty space next to a disgustingly large jar of mayonnaise. She released the handle of the refrigerator door. A pause, and then:

"Yes, of course I misplaced it. God knows I never keep anything in order around these parts—" Oh, god, Rich thought, "—like when the rats were about and I thought we should train them to clean up after us like some kind of circus tamer. Is Joseph about?"

"Yes, he's starting the children off on their Satanism class early today."

"Be serious, Rich. Humorless people get farther in life."

"He's out with the kids playing in the backyard."

"My backyard isn't big enough for all those children."

"They must be coming in then."

"Good job, Rich. With a little more experience you will make a wonderful secretary to a shepherd."

"I'm practically drowning in the potential, Netty."

Nanette resorted to opening and closing the cabinets around the kitchen in hopes of exhuming a lunchbox. She didn't know if she liked the nickname Netty. Once she overheard Rich referring to her as Headmistress Abbot, poking fun at her puritanical compulsions and her ineptitude for the easygoing, and she couldn't help but forlornly miss that title with slight yearning of what could've been.

"Did you pick up my prescription?" Nanette asked.

"Joey did. It's on your sink."

"And I got that brie you wanted from the deli last night. Did you see?"

"I did. Can't wait to dig into it."

Then in swarmed the kids, ricocheting faster than Nanette could care to count.

There was Jon, the oldest at nine years old, who grew his hair out to look like his mother's. Then there were Zola and Virginia, the twins of five years, who insisted on bringing in their own Lego bricks every day to innovate on past designs. Roux, who was eight, didn't seem to know how to talk but her baby brother, Pax, who at three and a half and only knew about a handful of words, never managed to shut up. Pax was the youngest of the bunch and Yuki, the second youngest at four, was his best friend. Yuki—being an only child—latched onto the friendship of Roux and Pax on her first day as a Baby Badger. Then there was Figgy, who renamed herself before Joey had the chance to remember her real name; there was Javier, the newest addition to the daycare and struggled to learn the ropes; and Meadow, whose need to be the worldliest kid in the room emphasized her parents' money. These three made up the largest group of same-aged kids, coming in at seven years old for each of them. Then there was a tenth child, but he or she had only ever really been known as The Tenth Child (also known as Tenth Child, The Tenth Child, or just 'Tenth' seeing as the nickname was also something no one person was able to specify): their mother dropped them off late and picked them up early, they kept to their self most of the time, watching, as if to figure out what it meant to be human. And thus the roster was set: the core collection of children was that of Jon, Zola, Virginia, Roux, Pax, Yuki, Figgy, Javier, Meadow, and The Tenth.

In the center of the oncoming storm stood Joey Abbot, the tolerated cousin of Nanette. He was a taller fellow with shorter hair, built in ways that made it easy for him to carry several overenthusiastic children at once. Usually a button-down shirt enthusiast, Joey forewent the style in the summer months for the simplicity of tank tops and jeans, often with his beloved button-downs tied around his waist. He was the most sedentary of the Abbot family, and the easiest to get along with. The titan towered above the tiny humans carrying Yuki in his arms as he called out, "Everyone go wash your hands! No eating until you get cleaned up."

One more thing to note about Joey Abbot: for, oh, four or five months now he's had the velvet box of an engagement ring weighing him down as he waited for the perfect moment. That moment of which he confidently believed was any day now.

He set down the little girl as the kids stampeded into the bathroom chanting "Garden, garden, garden!" and chuckling as if one had made a joke.

Joey waltzed through the kitchen and rinsed his own

hands in the kitchen sink, the wringing of his hands slowed down as he grew more and more conscious of Nanette's unannounced presence until he held his unmoving hands under the current. Knowing she was looking at him, he spoke.

"Good to see you, Nanette. Didn't expect to see you in the middle of the day."

"My lunchbox seems to have forgotten me."

"That's unlike you."

"Hmm, yes."

"Have you checked the refrigerator?"

"Oh no. Completely slipped my mind. Just got finished digging through all the plant pots—perhaps I will try the refrigerator next."

"We can spare a sandwich if you need a lunch."

"It is ham and cheese day."

"I'm sure you—"

"Please, Joseph."

"You must not have long for your lunch hour, though."

Rich interjected, "Well, she has the standard hour."

"Did you, either of you," Nanette cut in, "move my lunchbox?"

"And risk the inquisition?" Joey scoffed. "No."

"Well then you won't mind if I check downstairs."

"Why would you need to check downstairs? If it's not in the fridge, then maybe you left it at work yesterday. Do you remember even making a lunch for today?"

"I definitely brought the lunchbox home with me last night. It is ham and cheese day. I am speaking English, yes?"

Rich stepped in between the cousins, a jar of marshmallow fluff in hand. He smiled in that way he always did that made Joey step back. Joey, by nature, relaxed against the counter, shoulders loose. Nanette remained upright and the tapping of her foot matched the time running out of her lunch hour. It's true, she didn't have the time to search the house for her lunchbox but, also true, she'd rather stand in the middle of a leper orgy than eat a peanut butter sandwich on ham and cheese day. However, Joey, in the young, conceited way of boys, would not be able to have Nanette's level of empathy—she was sure.

Seconds passed. Rich kept unscrewing and screwing the lid to the jar. Nanette's eyes sized up the boys. Little Javier came into the kitchen and immediately Joey said, "Javy, do those hands look clean to you?" The crestfallen youth returned to the bathroom.

The other nine children flooded the kitchen, scuttling their way to the huge dining room table—which really was just two regular tables pushed together—and loudly waited. Pax and Yuki, being the shortest of the bunch, stood on the seats of the chairs raucously discussing the weather as if they knew what a warm front was.

"Looks like we're finally gonna get some rain!" Pax blurted, as if it was the only thing he'd ever heard. And that was Nanette's ultimate cue to go. With a huff, she pushed off to the door for the garage.

"Everyone say hi and bye to Miss Nanette," Joey announced and the kids listened, replying incongruously. Rich scurried to the door and opened it for Nanette.

Aside to her, Rich said, "If we find it, we'll let you know."

"Thank goodness," she said. "To think you'd keep such an earth-shattering secret to yourselves." And she disappeared behind the door.

Joey and Rich darted a glance to each other, agreeing on the oddity of the situation but ultimately not worrying about it. Joey started delivering the sandwiches to the kids whose parents hadn't sent them off to Baby Badger with lunches. For instance, Jon, raised by only his mother, used to send him off to Baby Badger every day with some salad until Joey offered to help her out by just cooking for the boy there. Other kids had loftier dietary restrictions, like Zola and Virginia who were both gluten free. Pax can't eat pollen, which was his way of saying he was allergic to pollen, but still it was good information for Joey to have.

As he watched the kids with lunchboxes unpack their meals, Joey considered how easily one of the kids could have confusedly swapped theirs for Nanette's. Sure, hers wasn't as whimsical as the Paw Patrol designs on the kids' lunchboxes (Nanette's was dotted with green and yellow hexagons, which to her actually may be a whimsical design). But even if that was the case, Nanette would've walked off with a lunchbox that wasn't hers rather than no lunchbox at all. Joey and Rich took their seats at either side of the table. Because the kids tended to stick with the same spot from day to day, the guys liked to switch off the end they sat at. Today Rich was with the seven-year-olds, Figgy, Javier, and Meadow, and Joey sat by Pax, Yuki, and Roux. The twins, Zola and Virginia, had long given up trying to make conversation with The Tenth but Jon's easygoing ways left him to share what little of his sandwich he had left with The Tenth just in case they were still hungry. As he pulled out his chair, Joey ruffled the deep red hair on Roux's head. She smiled as she chomped into her sandwich.

Joey liked all the kids, though he knew Roux's parents the longest. He'd known the Fieldings since he was in high school. The father opted out of college in favor of working at his uncle's dealership while their mother was working to get her doctorate in education. They stayed close seeing how Doctor Fielding and Joey went to the same college and the two couples hung out doing various activities. Joey had known Roux long enough to know exactly what she meant even if she wasn't able to say it. In times of emergency, the little girl would write on a piece of paper but for the most part that was unnecessary.

On the other end of the table, Rich was trying to get Meadow to put her phone away. He didn't know how her father could allow her to have an iPhone at her age but he did know that the rule was no phones at the table. "I needed to show Javier something!" she protested. And when Rich asked Javier what it was he needed to see, Javier just replied, "I dunno." Upon failure to put it away, Rich confiscated the phone like he did at least once a week. Meadow often threatened when this happened. She'd tell her dad, she'd say. And she has, often. The thing was, Joey and Rich were friends with all the children's parents beforehand and Meadow's father was always too distracted or too busy to reprimand his daughter's caretakers on her whim. The guys were the youngest of all their friends—some of them already being fully realized adults when Joey was just graduating high school.

But in truth, most of the kids were wholesomely good kids.

Lunch wrapped up. The kids with lunchboxes packed up and stored them in the cubbies near the front door on the landing. Joey picked up Pax—knowing he'd be the most difficult—and announced that it was naptime. The kids groaned, understandably.

"Do we have to?" Figgy asked, assuming the role of the voice of the people.

"We do this every day," Joey laughed. "To the nap room, everyone."

"But we shouldn't have to if we're not the babies."

"None of you are the babies."

"I'm a baby," Pax clarified.

"You want to take a nap, mister?"

"No. But still."

Then, to the room, "The only one who doesn't need a nap is Jon because he's the oldest."

Coolly, Jon replied, "I'm okay with a nap. My sister's in college and she said I'll miss them."

Joey knew that would be Jon's response and led the procession into the nap room. In truth, most of the kids were too old for naps, Roux, the seven-year-olds, maybe even The Tenth Child, it was fortunate for Joey and Rich though that the kids had not yet realized this and were still willing to nap after lunch each day.

The nap room was just the playroom with the yoga mats all rolled out.

In the corner near the sliding door, Roux pulled the shades closed on the windows because it was her most enjoyed job. She took charge of Pax and Yuki and tucked them into their own mats before settling down. Rich saw to it that there was always space to put Zola and Virginia next to each other as well as a space for Virginia to put her prosthetic foot without it "walking off." (This was Virginia's favorite joke and so she told it daily.) Figgy lay between Javier and Meadow to keep Meadow from poking Javier with her foot. Jon found a spot not far from Yuki because he was developing his first crush on Roux and couldn't understand his want to be close to her resulting in him sleeping at the feet of toddlers. Joey and Rich met at the door before turning out the light and, as usual, the last thing they saw was The Tenth sitting straight up in the middle of the room.

Joey closed the door behind them. Together, the guys took their afternoon breath. He put his arm around Rich and pulled him close, bestowing a weighted kiss on his forehead. In their work there was a drought of soft and intimate moments. Nanette was usually home before the last child got picked up for the day, so they never had the house to themselves. Rich and Joey never expected to go into childcare; they were just naturals at it. They loved the kids even if they only looked after them to give the parents a break. Well, that's how it started at least.

So naptime was its own blessing. On occasion, they would take a nap as well. In honesty, today was a good contender for a nap granted by an impromptu Nanette arrival. But, no. Today was a "harvest" day, as Rich wished Joey didn't call them. These were days when, for moments at a time, Rich and Joey would go into the "garden" to get the extra work done. Walking on the pads of their feet, they'd walk past the carpeted stairs and dip into their bedroom, hand in hand. Then one of them would break away. Today it was Joey, who went to their closet and—accustomed to the vibrant blue glow—would toss open the door, casting the room into an electric luminosity of the grow lights concealed within. They never got to spend much time together, just them, so a shared interest in gardening helped their relationship.

Whenever they needed to discuss something pressing, the boys would announce they had to talk in the garden about something the children weren't supposed to know.

Rich put on some Chopin at a soft volume, as not to disturb the kids, and the guys went to work. The closet was a walk-in, but they kept their clothes in wardrobes and on racks at the other side of the room. In the closet sat two large tents, each with a number of cannabis stalks rising from the soil. On the far wall of the garden, simply because there was the space, hung a couple framed photographs of Nanette and Joey when they were kids and of Rich and Joey at graduation.

The boys didn't smoke nearly as much as they used to. In fact, they hadn't for months at this point. They hadn't the time, what with the daycare and all. Not to mention there was the inability to have peace when Nanette was out of her room or her office. The only thing that really seemed to stick around from their younger stoned days was Joey's need to have a scented candle going. Today's scent was fresh cotton.

Rich pulled out the box of Ziploc bags and the scale and Joey started filling up their orders. In a blink, the alarm went off alerting them naptime was nearly adjourned and they started cleaning up as quick as they could.

Joey wasn't paranoid any more than he needed to be: if Nanette found out about the Baby Badger Cub Club's secret garden then it would surely be the end of everything. He and Rich would need to find a new place to live that could sustain a daycare (unless Nanette went to the police, and then their troubles might be a smidge grander). But Joey understood his cousin better than her own parents. They were members of that section of the Abbots who were rather humane and would've been snappy to offer Joey a place to stay if Nanette hadn't collected him and Rich with such expedience. Though good (and relatively normal) people, (considering the fact they'd spawned Nanette) the Abbots would not have also accepted Rich, who was just as terrified entering the working world without the help of his parents. Joey mastered recognizing the important habits of his cousin and built the business around them, which was why he'd be lying if the disappearance of her lunchbox wasn't a source of stress. She didn't slip up like this. Nanette Abbot was an overly efficient person, with more emphasis on the efficient than on the person.

"I know I tell you this every day, sweetie," Rich said, compelled, "but your cousin is a loon."

"Ha, yeah," Joey nodded.

"Suppose she lost her lunchbox?"

"It's more likely a wormhole opened and sucked it up."

"We have to move out of this house."

"And go where?"

Moving out of Nanette's home had been a goal for their relationship since they had moved in, and had discussed the prospect any time a paycheck made it their way.

"I dunno. But somewhere else."

"It'd make this big house awfully quiet."

"That wouldn't be our problem."

"Awfully quiet."

With all the gardening cleaned up, with five minutes to spare, the boys went to wake up the children. Rich poked his head in and, as usual, he saw the dim silhouette of The Tenth still sitting upright in the middle of the room not making a fuss, just breathing a little louder than the rest of the children. Asthma, he hoped.

"Afternoon arts and crafts time," Rich announced, with a smile.

And with the consistency of a clock's tick-tock, the kids put away their blankets and mats and followed Rich upstairs to the arts and crafts area.

The normal routine continued, after the Nanette hiccup. It was about 3:30 p.m. when the doorbell rang and Joey found Jenny Savoy there, a lithe and jolly woman who used to go by Persephone in school. Her hair was a collection of golden ringlets kept out of her eyes with a mauve headband. The daffodils of her dress failed to overpower the sunshine of her hair. Jenny and Joey dated briefly in middle school but fell out of touch since they were freshmen. This was obviously before the onset of Joey's sexuality. In that time, though, through Jenny and Joey's estrangement, Jenny had managed to find a husband of whom Joey had never seen or learned the name. She kept her own surname in the marriage.

"Hey, Jen," Joey beamed. "Right on time. Would you like a snack?"

"Not today," Jenny grinned. "Maybe tomorrow, though. Gotta get home to the ol' ball and chain."

"Okay." He glanced behind himself to see if Rich was nearby. Rather than Rich, Joey found The Tenth standing behind him, noiselessly, as was to be expected. To the child, he said, "Ready to go home?"

Nodding, The Tenth floated through the front door and took their mother's hand.

"Same time tomorrow?" Joey asked.

"Yessir. I think you have a new neighbor!"

"Oh?"

"There's a li'l turtle crossing the street."

"I'll have to check it out."

"Don't miss it! And don't think I won't follow up on that snack."

"Please do," he chuckled, sending them on their way.

Heading up the stairs, Joey laughed to himself. He didn't know why. He didn't know what was so funny. He heard the excited shrieks of the kids, the squeaking of chairs being pulled out and pushed in, a distant television that someone neglected to shut off; he heard Rich giving the kids instructions; he heard the birds bringing in the early summertime; he heard the lawnmowers of the neighbors; and he heard the traffic not too far. There was the whir of the air conditioning and the flush of a toilet. And in the back—the very back—of his head there was the voice of Nanette nagging him. But as the afternoon sunlight beamed into the house, illuminating the arts and crafts or blinding the children (depending on the side of the table they sat on), Joey laughed and laughed but couldn't help but wonder what, what, what, was so funny...

CHAPTER TWO

AU CONTRAIRE

Later that day, only two kids remained at Baby Badger: Roux and Pax Fielding. As was the case when the whim took to their parents, Mister and Doctor Fielding stayed for a quick drink as Joey prepared them a snack. The two parents brought a nice summery breeze into the house with them. The friendship between Joey and the Fieldings ran farther back than his relationship to any other of the Baby Badgers' parents, so much so that the origin of the friendship has been diluted by time and obscured by several people claiming different tales. What remained constant between stories was that Joey was consistently self-conscious about his friends, even though they were much older, having children and being married, in addition to Mister and Doctor Fielding being consistently self-conscious about Joey being so young and having so much of his life ahead of him. Over the years, the friendship finally unified all concerned parties helping in the childhood of the same kids and, thus, rendered them equally without energy.

At any given moment, these were the facts that Rich could recall about the Fieldings. Most of the parents were Joey's friends in some capacity and, though remarkably personable people, he often felt left out of the conversation.

Rich held no notion as to how Joey had so many friends with children at their age, after all they were both only twenty-four. Rich's friends were all just settling into jobs that loosely pertained to their major, let alone ready for families. And at least with the Fieldings he could relax in the knowledge that they were among the more normal of the children's parents. For Rich, many of them were closer to a source of income than to a source of friendship.

He took a sip from his chardonnay, feeling his shoulders lax, and admired that it was the part of the year when the sun lingered longer into the night.

"Of all things," Joey said to the group, "Nanette forgot her lunch today."

"Well, that's unlike her," said Doctor Fielding. "Is this it? Is she finally unhinging?"

"We'll see," said Rich, taking another sip.

"She's probably fine," Joey assured. "No person's perfect."

"Yes, but a machine can get pretty close," Al said into his drink.

Joey chuckled. But then he couldn't stop himself from noticing that his thumb kept tracing the rim of his glass. He put the drink down and sidled up beside Rich. They switched conversation to chat of the kids. It was the same update every day for the Fielding children: so kind, so well-behaved. The only incident of late with Roux was when she pushed Meadow aside in retaliation for Meadow trying to pull a hello out of her. Rich would story the escapades of Pax and Roux and their friend (Oh, I know this! It's that Yuki Yukimura…Yuki Shimizu girl… That Yuki—Her last name is Green, Al) Yuki as they would pretend to be pirates or penguins or exist in an imaginary *Minecraft* world. And regardless of the nonsense, everyone was just glad the kids were socializing.

When it came time, the Fieldings put their glasses in the sink, paid Rich for the day's services, and went to collect their children. The grownups all knew the various hiding spots that the kids could be in; only a few places in the house were off-limits: Nanette's room, Nanette's office, Nanette's garage (which was really the shared garage but it saved time referring to it as hers). And so it only took moments to find them in the upstairs living room, Pax sleeping in his sister's arms and Roux looking like she really needed the bathroom. Al scooped up his son as his daughter scurried off. He moved with a slight, calming bounce in his gait as his wife fished the car keys out of her purse.

The garage door then rumbled open and Nanette's car groaned up the drive.

The adults all paused, listening to the telltale signs of a car door shut and then the plodding footsteps of Nanette Abbot skitter up the stairs and plow into the kitchen. She was grunting and groaning to the point that Joey could feel her exasperation through the walls. Nanette came into the living room.

"Oh, the Fieldings are still here. Splendid," Nanette said, and then added under her breath: "I was worried I might not have gotten a moment of peace today."

Doctor Fielding coughed, and said, "Have a rough day, Miss Abbot?"

"Rough? Well, if we want to dilute the vocabulary for the sake of the kids. My day was a disaster. First, my lunchbox is lost."

The room waited a few moments for her to continue on as they watched Nanette breath profoundly and stare at the ceiling.

Joey asked finally, "And then?"

"Then what?"

"What happened after that?"

"Well, I didn't have a lunch then, didn't I?"

"It just sounded like there was a list."

"No there didn't."

"Yes," Rich added, "you said 'First'. Like there was more."

"I did not."

"I heard it," said Doctor Fielding. "Did you, dear?"

"Yes."

"I did not!" Nanette shrieked. "How could anyone possibly continue on after something as tragic as a lost love—" she coughed "—sorry, a lost lunch? Anything after that may have just debilitated me and that would never have happened because I am the only competent one around here. So, speak up. Did anyone else here think I started saying a list? Hmm?"

Pax, picking his tired head up from his father's shoulder, said, "Yes, I did."

Silence.

Some more silence.

And then: "Okay! Roux, out of the bathroom," said Al, going to the door. "We're going home, sweetie, come on!"

"Roux!" Doctor Fielding went into the bathroom and came out carrying her daughter. "Shame we couldn't stay longer."

"Don't forget your snack," said Joey as he ushered them out the door.

He turned to Nanette and Rich, "Well that was—"

"Honestly! What kind of rude, plebian children are you helping raise, Joseph? For the sake of . . . of goodness! I work hard every single day to keep a house over all of our heads, only to come and receive the third degree from a toddler. Look at him toddle his way into a life of unmitigated rudeness." She chuckled then, as if thinking her last sentence particularly clever. "The insensitivity! As if the child never knew the tragedy of losing something as dear as a lunchbox. Ha! Ha!"

"*Au contraire*," Rich said.

"Pardon?" Nanette said.

Rich, with all his fear for the day exhausted, flushed from his system, decided that he'd met his Netty quota. "*Au. Contraire.*"

"What are you saying?"

Joey piped in. "It's French. It means like 'to the contrary,' I think. That kid might actually know something about the tragedy of a missing lunchbox."

"*Au contraire?*" Nanette echoed. "Doesn't sound French."

"How does it not?" Rich, who majored in French, asked.

"Bistro. Now that's French."

"Maybe because it's Italian."

"*Au contraire*," Nanette proclaimed. "If that child does know something about my lunchbox, how do you suppose I would find out?"

This gave Joey pause. He didn't know what brain-goblin in Nanette's head thought he meant that Pax had information on Nanette's lunchbox. Joey meant that Pax probably knew what it was like to lose something like a lunchbox. Why would a half-asleep three-point-five-year-old know anything about this thirty-something-year-old's missing lunch?

"I meant *a* lunchbox. Not *your* lunchbox."

"Why would I care about some extraneous lunchbox?"

"I thought it might imbue some empathy."

"Well, you have failed. If anything, you seem even more apathetic to my plight."

"Yes, that's exactly what I meant, Nanette."

Nanette took a step back and, for the first time today, thought something through. Joey and Rich, though arguably decent people, were far too incompetent to uncover the perp of the great lunchbox caper. But Nanette wasn't. Any one of those rude, plebian children could just as easily stolen that lunchbox because they liked the colors or the material or because they knew it was ham and cheese day and Rich had made peanut butter sandwiches like a rube. She wouldn't put it passed her that there was a sliver of a chance that it was 100 percent likely that a child had stolen her lunchbox.

But she wouldn't have to start investigating the children if the box was still in the house.

Nanette, mid-conversation, ducked into the bathroom. There was a narrow closet filled with towels and toilet paper out of which she began pulling things. She never used this bathroom because it was one of the ones that the boys and the kids used. Even now, after only touching the doorknob, Nanette felt compelled to wash the stickiness off her hands. Rolls of toilet paper and the stray hand towels plopped down into a disheveled pile atop the off-white ceramic tile. After the closet was empty, Nanette crawled over to the shower and pulled back the curtain. She found the laundry hamper the boys hid in there for the work day and dumped it onto the floor. By then, Rich, being the person he anticipated to clean up the mess, intervened.

He hooked himself around Nanette's shoulders and lifted her to her feet. Nanette pushed herself away from Rich and said, "No need to be so drastic," as she brushed herself off.

"Nanette," Joey said, stepping into the bathroom, "why would your lunchbox be in the bathroom?"

"Good question, very good question," Nanette scoffed. "But answer me this: why *would* my lunchbox be in the bathroom? Are you hiding it from me? Having a laugh at poor Nanette, are we?"

"Yes, we are," Rich said. "We are having a big old laugh right now because nothing gives us more pleasure than squirreling away a stupid roast beef sandwich!"

"It's *ham and cheese* day! You sound ridiculous—mocking me."

"Rich," Joey said, "step back, please. Netty, why would we take your lunchbox?"

"Jealousy."

"Jealous of your lunchbox?"

"How should I know! Sure. Yes. To keep me humble, you stole my lunchbox. And after everything I have done for the both of you. I took you in. I gave you two a home. And now you, you, you are laughing at me behind my back."

Under his breath Rich whispered, "Not necessarily behind it."

"You can't bring up your charity every time something goes wrong, Netty," Joey said.

"Why not? It is my house. I have a right to do with it as I please. I can search every corner if I darn well choose to."

"You can't just search every corner," Rich stated.

"Why? Hiding something, like a lunchbox?"

"Okay so you want to search every corner? Wanna go

through my extensive collection of boxer briefs?"

"Of course not."

Nanette understood that something precious like her lunchbox was so much better than any one thing to be kept in a drawer with a man's unmentionables. But who was to say that Rich wouldn't hide it with his shirts? Or his ties? Granted that bohemians like Richard Eliot and Joseph Abbot even owned any ties. However, it would be the strongest guess for a hiding spot. Nanette cocked her head and smiled.

"You are right, I am overreacting a bit. You understand. How about you guys go about your night and I will clean up in here?"

"Sounds good," Joey said.

Nanette watched the boys lumber out of the bathroom then turn to go down the hall, and with their backs turned to her, Nanette darted down the staircase. She forgot how to make her feet move quietly so the immediate pummeling of her shoes against the steps sounded like a lunatic falling down stairs. She got to Rich and Joey's bedroom. Barreling in she repeated "tie drawer" over and over and over again until it was just indiscernible nonsense. *Tiedrawer tijer tijrawer tietiegier.* The bedroom was pretty much the same since the last time she'd seen it: the bed central in the room, the walls lined with a couple wardrobes and racks for their button downs and jackets. At the far wall was the walk-in closet and beside that door was the desk that Rich and Joey did the books for the daycare. They didn't have an office, especially seeing how most of the rooms in the house were repurposed for children.

By the time Nanette had rushed across the landing on the staircase, Joey was at the top of the stairs in pursuit, and Rich was still turning around halfway through asking, "What was that?"

Nanette threw open the doors to one of the wardrobes in hopes of finding the ties. She dug around in a pile of dress shoes, disgracefully disorganized, still repeating the same two words. Not wise to his presence, Joey appeared between her and the wardrobe. Startled, she backed up and fell over onto the bed.

Rich appeared in the doorway. Sitting up, Nanette shouted, "Proof! It's in here somewhere, isn't it?"

"You're crazy," was Rich's retaliation.

"If I am so crazy then what's my lunchbox doing in your closest?"

"Wuh-oh," Joey vocalized.

Nanette lunged for the closet door but came up short because, moving fast, Joey grabbed onto her ankle forcing her to fall face down onto the carpet. Panicked and tiptoeing, Rich ran across the room and blocked Nanette from the closet door.

"It's not in the closet," Rich's voice cracked.

"If it's not there, then why can't I just look?"

"Because…"

"Because," Joey picked up, "there is a . . . a naked sculpture of Rich—not of Rich, of me. There's a naked sculpture of me in there, which is weirder because we're cousins, and you wouldn't want to see that because it's . . . it's too realistic. Just too damn realistic. And do you want to see all that . . . all that stuff?"

"A sculpture—?! Who is making a naked sculpture of you?"

"Arts and crafts project!" Rich blurted.

"What?" Nanette was horrified. "Like with the children?"

"No!" said Joey. "Just a regular, grownup art project. Nothing seedy with the children."

"And you're just keeping it in the closet?"

"Where else would we keep something?"

"Well, fine." Nanette picked herself up off the ground. She looked at the top of their shared desk and rifled through some of the papers and the jar they had filled with pens. She opened a desk drawer revealing a box filled with Ziploc bags and a scale, thought nothing of it, and shut it again. "That is that for now."

"That's that for now," Joey echoed.

Walking to the doorway, Nanette said ultimately, "I like the color you painted the walls here."

She was gone, left to resume her usual beat. Joey and Rich collapsed onto the bed, one on top of the other. Joey, the taller of the two, tended to end up under Rich whenever this would happen. Ten, twenty minutes passed with the two just staring up at the popcorn ceiling, listening to the uniform footsteps of Nanette reverberate like the *Jaws* theme. Joey could feel the tender moments when Rich would fall asleep, waking up minutes later acting like no time had passed. They were more tired now than they ever had been before. Were they not young? Were they not enterprising?

They shared a bedroom in the basement of a house they didn't own, watching after kids that weren't theirs. And one "kid" was thirty-two years old. But then again, a couple of virile young lads like themselves should be out on the town in these golden years, crashing cars and womanizing. Joey wondered how it had come to this. He was reluctant to move in with his cousin full-time. But toward the end of his college days he needed a place to stay for a couple of weeks and Grandmother Abbot had initially twisted Nanette's will into opening up for him. Those final months in school had blinked by.

It was around the time his parents had kicked him out. He hadn't told them that he was gay, and he didn't know how they could've found out, but when they presented the question "Are you or aren't you" well, his parents didn't raise a liar now, did they? Nanette, almost eager, or as eager as one could fathom Nanette being, took him in. Took Rich in, too. And then complained about it for two years straight. Joey was afraid of those days, the helpless, directionless days, and the idea of a return was exasperating. He never told this to Rich nor Netty, but he wondered if they could read it on his face.

With Rich around his waist, Joey slowly reached to turn out the lights. Fully clothed, on top of the covers, the men, then, fancied a nap.

Of course she knew how many tiles were in her ceiling; she

counted them at least three times every night before going to sleep. Thirty-two and five-eighths tiles. There was the same number of tiles as there were years that Nanette had been alive. She never stayed up this late. It must've been at least 10:30 p.m. and she was staring up at her bedroom ceiling wasting away like some midnight debauching philanderer.

One tile, two tiles, three tiles, four…

Perhaps this night life was personable to Joseph and Richard but it just didn't tickle Nanette, that was for darn sure. She lay on the right side of her king size bed, like she did every night. She didn't roll in her sleep, she didn't dream, she simply closed her eyes and then it was morning. But not tonight. Too many things had gone awry. First, her lunchbox went missing.

All the people that breezed through her house daily: some of them were kids, others most likely corrupt parents—PTA backwash that sold upstanding citizens' lunchboxes on the black market with some mendicant's kidney inside. It was a sham of a Monday, all these thieving youths would be back tomorrow. Some of them, she thought, were far too old for the services of the daycare. The one boy with the girl hair, he must've been nine years old—what's he doing out of school and in the Baby Badger Cub Club? His parents were the obvious candidates for fleecing the daycare out of its hard-earned lunchboxes.

Sixteen tiles, seventeen, eighteen…

Nanette was a good person. She donated to charity when they'd backed her into corners. She opened up her house for the needy. At least she did when she was yelled at by Grandmother Abbot, the only truly scary woman in the world. She bought groceries, cleaned up, and put a roof over her cousin's head and she didn't even hold that over him. Never once. So, what was the deal with this sudden hiccup in the Universe? The hole that opened up and swallowed her lunchbox *whole*? Where was the justice in being? The karma? The what goes around comes around?

Au contraire, she thought, *au contraire*.

There was a thief walking the halls. She didn't care if they were sixty-six or three and a half. Nanette Abbot would find them and . . . she wouldn't make them pay but, oh they better believe it, they'd receive a stern, stern lecture.

Twenty-nine, thirty, thirty-one…

Au contraire. Now that really didn't sound like French, did it?

CHAPTER THREE

FIGGY ALLAWAY

Mister Rich, even though he tried so hard, was never able to get the hang of the seven-year-olds. Mister Joey understood that the sevens were what they were and that wasn't about to change, so that made him cool.

The sevens were Figgy Allaway, Javier Bolivar, and Meadow Descoteaux and the power dynamic was always in flux. Javier, who was the newest addition to the Baby Badgers, was always trying to learn how things worked around here. Like when Mister Joey and Mister Rich needed to keep secrets, they would go to the garden and so whenever one of the Badgers kept a secret, they too went to the garden. But because Javier just wanted to fit in, he had no power—which in a roundabout way gave him the most power. The two girls, though admittedly best friends, were constantly struggling to have the final say in the group's activities. If Meadow wanted to paint Pax's face, Figgy wanted to clean up. When Figgy had a snack, she shared; when Javier had a snack, Meadow took half. Javier never realized that the three of them ended up doing what he wanted because if Figgy wanted to do it, the group had agreed, but if Meadow wanted to do it then she took credit.

Today Figgy didn't have the energy to combat Meadow. Something wasn't quite right ever since yesterday when Miss Nanette showed up at lunch and seemed to jinx the whole atmosphere. This morning, her dad needed to swerve out of the way of a turtle crossing the street before clambering into the driveway and Figgy knew, just knew, that something was off in the world. So she sat back, using her shirt to clean her glasses, watching Javier and Meadow pretend to buy a house. They were sharing the playroom with the twins, Zola and Virginia, and also The Tenth. Zola had flipped over one of the plastic kick-powered cars and somehow Virginia had found a way to remove the tires. Those girls were in the process of switching around all the tires on the car as The Tenth watched wordlessly. Figgy noted how the sky out the window seemed more purplish today and she didn't think she liked it even though she knew there was nothing she could do.

"I can't believe your cousin is staying with us," Meadow said, gesturing to the quiet Figgy. "She should get a real job you know."

"Yes, dear," Javier said, then added, "Figgy's not my cousin."

"I know, Javy, it's part of the game."

Javier wasn't interested in the game if he didn't think everyone was for it. But he also didn't know if Figgy's distance was part of the game after all. As if to test this uncertainty, Javier poked Figgy in the arm and hazarded, "Hey, get a job."

"Wha?" Figgy looked up, putting her glasses back on. "Job?"

"Yeah, a job," Meadow commanded.

"I'm a soldier," Figgy said.

"You can be a librarian."

"But I want to be a soldier."

"You can be a soldier," Javier assured.

"But, dear!" Meadow protested.

"Just let her be a soldier!"

In a daze, Figgy left the bickering couple behind her as she made a lap of the playroom. She traced her hand across the box with all the yoga mats, she patted the black mop of hair on The Tenth's head (an act they seemed to like as Figgy had been doing it for some time now), and then she walked by Zola and Virginia. Zola sat in the seat of the plastic car and said, "It's stallin'," as Virginia finished up the last of the wheels. Figgy told them it was looking good and continued on her walk. Before long, she was journeying up the carpeted steps to the living room that had the video games that the kids almost never got to play. And she wandered through the kitchen where Mister Rich was baking with Roux and Pax and Yuki. Jon was sitting at the table watching next to Mister Joey.

"Hey, Fig," said Mister Joey. "Javy and Meadow are downstairs."

"I know." She smiled half her usual amount.

"Everything okay, Fig?"

"Umm, okay, yeah."

Mister Joey turned to Jon and asked him if he'd be cool by himself for a little bit and Jon said that that was cool. He then took Figgy by the hand and asked her if she wanted to take a walk. She acquiesced. Mister Joey led her down the stairs to the garage, where Badgers only got to go to when they were getting special attention—a detail not lost on Figgy. Her grin perked up.

Joey could recognize happiness. Kids were their emotions. And Figgy was more happiness than most of her other feelings. Figgy savored the scent of the gasoline and the cut grass. She remembered the look of the push lawnmower in the corner and the random tubs stacked against the wall. Her shoes clicked against the wide concrete floor. *Tet-ta tet-ta.*

The garage door was open and the breeze nudged at Figgy's hair. She giggled, but not her full laugh.

"What's up, Figgy? You're not as chipper as usual."

"I don't know," she replied. "Some days are just more purple than other days."

Joey straightened his back. Though her words didn't make sense, they made perfect sense. Some days are just more purple than other days. He knew, immediately, that she would be fine. Figgy was an honest kid, a speak-what's-on-her-mind kid. Once she found out that Meadow had been sneaking bits of Javy's lunch to put in his shoes and she didn't even flinch letting anybody know. Sometimes there were kids like Jon, or Virginia, where one needed to be more tactful in figuring out.

"Need anything from me?" he offered.

"Yeah."

"What's up?"

"Could I get a hug?"

And so he got on one knee and threw his arms around her, picked her up and spun her around a couple times as she squealed with delight until Rich called down the stairs because the cake was ready.

It was inevitable that Nanette amassed over two months' worth of vacation days. Seeing how her job was almost entirely self-defined she trusted no one to be able to come and fill in. Even if whatever she needed to take time off for went over two months, her sick days would still stretch a fortnight. Rich described germs as "knowing better than to spend time with Nanette." When Nanette got in that morning, she booted up her laptop and opened up an Excel spreadsheet which went untouched for two whole hours.

Nanette's orthodox hyper-focus was off today. She had ended up doing nothing with the full intent of doing something. The miniature refrigerator in the corner housed, ludicrously, her lunch which was concealed by a classic brown paper bag. Joey had found them under the sink for her and it was begrudgingly a better solution than carrying the items by hand. The bag was a mockery and harkened back to the hand puppet fiasco of 2006, which was not important for Nanette to expound upon at this juncture. However, currently, she loathed the way the bag seemed to stain just by looking at it from certain angles. She hated the crinkle of the paper in her hand. She hated the evocative callback to a schoolyard recess—of which she had no pleasant memories.

Nanette's favorite part of her childhood was the fact she'd survived it.

She found that the kids she used to play with weren't capable of playing correctly, and when Nanette tried to teach them they retreated to their games of hide-and-seek like the true cowards they were. Her parents were no consolation either as they constantly forced the perspective of the other children onto her like some sort of misguided empathy tutorial. Nanette felt that she was as empathetic as she needed to be. They always told her that she would only be a kid once (and secretly worried that if she wasn't a kid in her youth then her childhood might come up in inopportune places, therefore never properly ending). The unbridled support and respect of personal space from her parents was absolutely suffocating. All Nanette, as a tiny human, ever wanted was strict protocol that she could learn, master, and then execute. The most formidable obstacle was her father's mother, Grandmother Norma Abbot, who too often critiqued how to properly be a child. So, as an act of rebellion, Nanette elected against friendships with the fellow children.

Even though Nanette thought about it, nearly obsessed about it, she didn't mourn the lack of being around other kids when she was young. She had used her lonely lunches to read or do homework so that when she got home she could do something fun, like read or do homework. She took notice that her oldest memories were of her youngest selves. But even then, in her collections of schoolyard thoughts, never once did she actually have a brown bag lunch.

She set to work. Opening up a separate spreadsheet, she filled out an entire column describing the children of the Baby Badger Cub Club as best she could remember them: Boy with mom hair, girl with singular foot, sister of girl with singular foot with standard amount of feet, redhead, won't shut up, girl, loud girl, smiley girl, boy, and shadow.

She preferred working here in her office at the firm rather than her office at home. She had a phenomenal view, of the parking lot. The walk to the bathroom was not that far. Her coworkers, though weeks would pass without a casual exchange, were amicable. Sometimes Nanette would walk by a group of laughing colleagues and join in the giggles even if she hadn't heard the joke. Once she told a joke herself and only three out of the five people walked away in silence. The remaining two just went back to talking about the funeral arrangements for an accountant's mother. In fact, the last major problem she had was when some degenerate thought he could identify which wood her desk was made out of: it was teak, Nanette knew this (even though it was actually mahogany). Nanette thought most wood that wasn't oak or pine was teak. Joey believed that this was because she only knows three types of wood and has been too proud to learn more.

There was a tap on her office door. Nanette slammed shut her laptop, lest some strange coworker be privy to her coveted spreadsheets. Before the person in her doorway could say anything, Nanette said, "Yes, what is it? Oh, you know what? Save it for tomorrow, I could use a good heart attack following another stealth mission you have seemed to pull on me. Look at the time—I must be off. Whatever you have for me leave it with Nina at the front desk, she gives me my messages. Where is my brief case? Shush, I know I'm holding it. Remember, Nina at the front desk. Yes, I know my lunch is in a paper bag—don't laugh at me."

Nanette scrambled to pack up her things and shut her office door before the person could get out a single syllable.

"Remember, Nina at the front desk."

The lunch bag felt like fire in her hand—bright, attention stealing, searing. She slung her messenger bag over her shoulder and with her free hand she hesitantly patted the person on the head before breaking for the elevator.

"But…" the person got out, dumbfounded, because she *was* Nina from the front desk. Nina wasn't awestruck by the effective train wreck of Nanette Abbot but she was concerned how far past lunch hour it was for Nanette to still have not eaten her food.

The receptionist wondered how that woman, who had won Employee of the Month three times in the past two years, managed. But at the same time, she wanted Nanette to "keep it together" until July because that's when she said in the office pool that Nanette would finally lose it for keeps. If she unhinges now, Turner in HR wins the bet and nobody, *nobody*, likes Turner enough to pay up.

Of the ten kids, only four of them remained to be picked up. It was about five o'clock and Joey had sent off people like Jenny Savoy with the snack he'd promised the previous day. As usual, the Fielding kids were still there, as was little Yuki, and Figgy Allaway. They all sat around with Mister Rich watching *The Lego Movie* on the big television in the living room upstairs.

Rich sat on the floor in front of the sofa with Pax in his lap and Roux to his side. Yuki wasn't interested in the movie, rather she was too engaged playing with Rich's hair. He let her have at it because his hair was relatively short and there was no damage she'd be able to inflict. Plus, he saw to it that all the crafts supplies were already put away so no one would be dyeing his hair with Crayola markers again anytime soon.

The purr of car tires pulled up the drive.

"Ohh, who's next?" Rich said. "Who's getting picked up?"

"Not me!" Pax almost cheered. He'd been talking throughout most of the movie but just about the things he saw in the film that he owned. Everyone knew *The Lego Movie* was a big commercial, and everyone kicked themselves for not thinking of it first. "My parents. Our parents are never first. SO, it's not us."

Then the garage door rattled open. Reflexively, Rich picked Pax up and set him aside as he began to rise. "No!" Yuki griped, trying to sit him back down so she could finish her creation.

"Tell me what I miss," Rich said as he hobbled into the kitchen. His left leg was asleep and he didn't realize it until he latched on to a counter for support.

Wide-eyed, Joey entered the kitchen. The men looked at each other, then at the door that led to the garage.

"Nanette's home?" Joey said.

"She's an hour early."

"She's an hour and thirty-three minutes early."

"What do we do?"

"Act natural. What's up with your hair? You look like a discount Danny Zuko."

"You don't like it?"

"Of course I like—"

The door swung open and, like a doe approaching kids with food in a petting zoo, Nanette crept into the kitchen. Obviously she hadn't expected the two boys to be there waiting for her. She clutched her messenger bag in front of her like it was a shield.

"Nanette," Joey said, "you're home early."

"Yes, this is true," she replied. "Phenomenal catch."

"Did work let out early at…?" Rich was constantly forgetting the fact that he didn't know where Nanette worked or what the name of the company was.

"I left early," she said sounding like a recorded message, "to pick up milk."

She faltered between not making eye contact and not breaking eye contact.

"Milk?" Joey repeated.

"Yes. Milk. And now I will lie down."

"O—" she left the kitchen, "—kay."

The doorbell chimed. Joey robotically left to receive it. It was probably one of the Allaways. They tended to be later on Tuesdays for whatever reason. And ever the consistent, Misses Allaway stood on the stoop with her well-rehearsed smile as Mister Allaway kept the pickup running in the street. Misses Allaway had untamable dirty blond hair that she kept up in a bun. She was in denim overalls with a tie-dyed T-shirt on underneath. Her right arm was completely covered in tattoos of her own design, animals and plants that she'd come to adore for some reason or another. At the top of her arm, a plentiful fig tree was tattooed there.

"Hey Beth," Joey said. "Reckon you wouldn't want to come in for a snack?"

"Not today, Joey," Misses Allaway returned, feigning a grin, "but we'll pay you for one before the week's out, I'm sure."

"Alright, just let me know. Figgy!" he called up the stairs into the house. "Your momma's here!"

Figgy appeared at the top of the stairs, scurrying down to collect her bag out of her cubbyhole by the door.

"Have fun today, Fig?" Misses Allaway asked.

"Yeah. Meadow made Javy get a job."

"Ah."

Joey and Misses Allaway exchanged their goodbyes and she arranged to pay him on Friday like most parents did. He watched them walk down the mason path to the street and Misses Allaway lifted Figgy up into the truck. Nanette popped out of her bedroom in a different jacket and crossed into the kitchen.

She and the boys all convened in the kitchen. Rich was naturally skeptical of Nanette's spontaneity, boldly questioned her.

"You're heading out?" Rich asked.

"I forgot the milk," she replied.

"The milk you just picked up?"

"Yes. Just plum forgot it."

"Forgot to buy it? Or forgot to bring it home?"

"Yesssssssssss. I forgot to bring it home. After. After I bought it, I left it at the store."

Joey, walking over to the refrigerator, opened it up and found an untouched gallon of 2 percent inside.

"We have milk," he said.

"Oh! Heaven forbid I am not allowed to spend my hard-earned salary on what I want. If I want more milk, I am going to get more milk. And also, we don't have every kind of milk—perhaps I am in the mood for skim? Huh? Does skim sound like an adventure in ridiculousness to you all? How about we all agree that milk can be purchased whenever and is of no concern, so even if tomorrow I need to go pick up milk, or the day after, then I goshdarned will do so. So, if you'll excuse me, I have to go buy some milk."

"Pick up milk," Rich clarified.

"Yes. Thank you."

And she slammed the door behind her.

Beth and Doug Allaway lived in an apartment that was refitted from an old mill building with their seven-year-old daughter, Augusta. If you were to ask Augusta what her name was she would say Figgy Allaway, quite adamantly. In fact, shortly after Figgy learned to talk, five years ago, among the first sentences out of her mouth was "Call me Figgy." Beth and Doug had little insight as to why their chirping baby girl had decided on her own title. Perhaps it was the orchard that Beth's father owned and the young couple retreated to when they had a spare couple of days. Or perhaps it was the fact that both of the Allaways had the compulsion to keep the kitchen stocked with figs. It had grown to be a need in the apartment that every day each member of the family had at least one fig. Even though, if pressed on why they ate so many figs, the Allaways would have no idea how to answer because, well, doesn't everyone eat this many figs?

Much to their displeasure, the Allaways were doing very well for themselves. Doug was a metalworker who took to sculpture at a young age. He hoped that at the end of his twenties he would still be in a crappy, urban, not-up-to-code piss-can of an apartment with five of his closest friends and one dude that they all collectively hated. Back after high school, when it was obvious to Doug that his academic work was pitifully irredeemable, his golden age of art had its expedient rise and collapse. His parents kicked him out for not going to college, he couldn't hold a job at the local supermarket, and there wasn't a passing day when he wasn't stoned to forget his problems. Suffice it to say, but he was a phenomenal artist.

Beth was a poet who had her associate's in whatever-it's-not-important-either-way. She'd met Doug at one of his gallery showings in a refitted warehouse that stank of urine and bird shit—it was so romantic. Beth graduated barely with a passing grade point average, opting to take a walk through scenic Massachusetts than to idealize academia through textbooks she never bought on principle. Since middle school, she had taken to painting and frequently found work as a stage painter. Beth was among the highest recommended stagehands in all of New England by the time she was twenty-two and seven months pregnant.

Doug, subject to the onset of love, got a steadier job with the city to support his soon-to-be wife during her pregnancy and—unfortunately—found to adore government work. Beth, all the same, after giving birth to Augusta Allaway, took three months of maternity leave before returning to the painting world. They loved their work, they loved each other, and they loved their daughter. Horrible, horrible love, that which made them feel light, untethered, unshackled to the drudgery of being with no comment to make, no stand to take. Just a dusty blowtorch, dried-up pen, and a kitchen filled with figs.

Horrible, horrible love.

Mister Allaway pulled into the parking lot of their apartment building, shambling into a usual spot. Misses Allaway helped little Figgy out of the truck's cabin. The little girl piggybacked onto her mother, half asleep, the mother headed for the front door of the old mill building with her slump-shouldered husband in tow. His expression neutral, head to the side, he watched contently as his wife spritely glided across the lot with his daughter on her wings.

Not too far behind them, a dark purple, immaculate car entered the parking lot. It swerved off of the street and punched the brakes upon seeing the three Allaways enter the building. Imagine a car tiptoeing, and that's what this one did to find a place to stop. What with time being of *the* essence, the car double parked in a couple of visitors' spaces. It backed up to try to pick just one of the spots, but just ended perfectly half-and-half over the yellow line.

Out stepped the suspicious Nanette Abbot.

Just shy of inaudible, Nanette whispered *The Pink Panther* theme song but with her own name as the lyrics. As she approached the Allaways' pickup truck, she sidled up to the car and peered inside. Nanette spied an old crushed McDonald's Happy Meal box and an empty-looking duffel bag. Save for some old water bottles in the cup holders, there was nothing of interest to Nanette in the cabin of the truck. Hoped it wouldn't come to this, she believed, but in life we're faced with certain inevitabilities.

Nanette walked into the old mill building and pulled on the inner glass door only to find that it wouldn't budge. On the side there was a panel of buttons next to labels of names of the people who lived there. Beside the buttons was a collection of holes in a metal panel that Nanette perceived to be a speaker. ALLAWAY—26, it read. She went to press it but stopped halfway. She wasn't here under friendly circumstances: this was espionage. The likeliness of the parents of the smiley girl recognizing Nanette's voice simply because of her preexisting popularity was too high that it would jeopardize everything.

Rather, she pressed number 25 and prayed.

"Yeah?" said a voice through a speaker.

"Hello," said Nanette.

A moment passed.

"What is it?" the voice grunted.

"I am down here."

"Are you here for my delivery?"

Nanette, not thinking herself a liberal liar, said, "I most certainly am not."

"Then what is it?"

Nanette paused for another moment.

"Oh... Did you say delivery? I thought you said paperboy."

"Right."

"We are always getting mixed up."

"Yeah okay. You want I should come down?"

"No, no, sir, I can bring it up."

Then the glass door began to buzz. Nanette flung it open and booked it for the stairs. The barren foyer of the mill building was tiled with what-she-couldn't-tell because everything was caked with dirt. The walls were covered with black and white, vintage photographs with a glass mosaic thrown in every couple steps. Pictures of canals and dogs and stained glass windows that looked like fire had an immense flair of artistry that Nanette found frivolous as she surmounted the steps.

At the top, she entered a corridor without a single soul. Muted rumors of televisions seeped through the whitewashed doors. Nanette walked on the pads of her feet, counting the doors going by: 20, 22, 24. She found her way to door 26 and held her ear up to the doorjamb. On the other side she could make out the discontented ramblings of a couple. Nanette backed away from the door and tried, though vainly, to spy through the peephole from the hallway side. As expected, all she saw was a miniscule white dot but, as unexpected, she pushed enough on the door for it to creep open a couple centimeters. The door hadn't been shut all the way.

Nanette held her hand over the brassy doorknob, finding the will to grab ahold, when something happened.

A man stepped out of the apartment across the hall. Sharply, Nanette spun to face him, snapping into place. He wore a T-shirt that didn't cover the bottom of his protruding stomach, which made her more uncomfortable than she thought she would be if someone had described to her this exact situation.

"You my delivery?" he asked.

"Umm, yes it would seem so."

"Where's the package?"

"In… the truck."

"Why didn't you bring it?"

"We wanted to know if you were here."

"You talked to me downstairs."

"That is exactly what I told them but they never listen to me. You know how it goes. Protocols and protocols. Corporate synergy and all that . . . jazz." She took a breath. "I'll go get that package."

"Yeah."

Nanette scooted back down the hall and hid around a corner until she saw the man retreat back into his apartment.

Meanwhile, Figgy lay in her bed for the night. It was a small room that was really meant to be a nursery. Young families tended to move to the suburbs by now when the parents' bohemian dreams went bust. Not that Figgy understood any of that. She listened to her parents talk through the wall—it was a lot of the same meanness from the night before. The night before had made her extremely uncomfortable, for the same reasons tonight was.

The noises through the wall bickered and bantered.

"Beth, I'm not comfortable with that place anymore. I never was."

"But Fig loves it there. She has friends. And Joey is good people, he needs the work and he knows kids."

"You're not supposed to mix kids with ... you know what I'm saying. They don't mix."

"Then we'll stop that, but not the daycare. She loves it too much. You know how traumatizing it can be without warning."

"We'll warn her."

"She's not leaving the daycare, Doug."

"We're not talking about this."

"You're right."

Figgy hopped out of her bed. She felt an intense need to move her legs so she decided to go for a glass of water. Her brain had memorized her bedroom. Though it was dark inside with the shades pulled, she knew where her dresser was, where her easel stood, where the corner of her rug liked to poke up and trip her dad when he wasn't looking. Figgy poked her head out the door.

She saw the living area, lit dimly by a single table lamp.

Her parents had moved into their bedroom by then so she snuck across the rooms, past the front door, into their little kitchen. The kitchen had two doors, one that connected to the hall and one to the living area. As Figgy made it into the kitchen, the front door swished open with Nanette's tentative visage sizing up the place.

The woman stepped in, making sure not to close the front door behind her completely. She needed to check the refrigerator. Nanette had decided early on that if a thief was to keep her lunchbox in any one place then it would be the fridge.

Figgy had a stepstool she put in front of the sink to reach it for water. Her parents bought it to help teach her independence and also because they were uncomfortable with her reaching in a room with quite a bit of knives.

Nanette entered the apartment stopping short. Down the hall she saw a tall metal sculpture that somehow looked like both an ostrich and a gallows. Though she didn't fully understand its meaning, what with its avant-garde employment of nuts and bolts, Nanette could glean enough to realize that whoever made it was definitely past their prime.

Figgy turned on the sink faucet as low as it would go, filling up her mom's *Thomas the Tank Engine* cup as quietly as possible. As she drank, she felt the cold stream fill her up and her worries quietened.

Nanette turned to her left and found a door that, presumably, led to the kitchen. The door was saloon style so she was able to see the tiles, but not much else. She went to go through them and as her foot hit the ground outside the kitchen Figgy dropped her cup into the sink and ran for the other egress, worried that that was her mother on the other side. The girl ducked into the living room as the resonant pitter-patter of her feet froze Nanette in place. They exhaled in unison.

Coming to, Nanette hustled into the kitchen and opened up the fridge while Figgy made a break for her bedroom door. The older woman quickly scanned the contents of the fridge to find a load of V8 juice and a lot of vegan nonsense.

Performing a fast 360 scan of the tiny kitchen, Nanette didn't find her lunchbox in the Allaway home. Crestfallen, she slumped.

Almost colliding, Figgy and Nanette met beside the front door of the apartment.

Silent, Figgy's face crescendoed into an unabashed smile as Nanette's fell open.

Figgy whispered, as loudly as she could without getting her in trouble, "Hi, Miss Nanette!"

Nanette, stumbling for the door, fell out of the apartment yelling, "Delivery! Delivery!"

CHAPTER FOUR

GRANDMOTHER

The week, much like everyone under the Abbot roof, persisted.

It was Wednesday morning marking the beginning of the third day that the lunchbox had been missing. Rich, who had a fitful rest, had been asking Joey what was stressing him out so badly, seeing how he spent the night rolling about in his sleep. Joey had grown into a calm, centered individual overall. Even if he was stressed with someone, it would rarely manifest itself into anxiety. It took an army to get a rise out of him and Rich knew this. Rich had spent years trying to figure out which buttons to press on Joey to get him bothered, irked, and miffed, with little success.

Of course, Joey got worried—in his line of work who wouldn't avoid a little daily freakout? But the only thing that had ever panicked him was back when his parents had kicked him out of the house after they had found out particular fun facts about him without him ever figuring out how they had acquired such (dubiously) fun facts. Additionally, whenever Nanette's habits were disrupted without warning, that was cause for some worry. The first time he ever experienced true, soul-chilling, ear-ringing fear was during the hand puppet fiasco of 2006—an event which gave him a point of reference for fear which most children use to define their traumas.

So as Joey stood at his shirt rack, paging through what would be his dress for the day, he didn't notice his tapping foot or his occasional tendency to consider the same shirt twice. But there was the inner drumming, something beside his heart, that made him pull out his phone and call Norma.

She would be up. Heck, she would have been up since 4:30 a.m. gardening or going through Facebook to see if anything changed within the family after she went to bed at seven the night before. Joey's grandmother was among his oldest friends in every sense of the word. She was this textbook sweet old lady as far as he knew. His whole life she would dole out affections and confections as she saw fit to her grandchildren, of which there were seven. There was Joey, who was an only child, and Nanette, who was an only child, but then there were the quintuplets: Ingrid, Alison, Ian, Maureen, and Lawrence who were known as Eeny, Meeny, Miney, Mo, and Larry, respectively. They were all among the relatives who had fallen out of touch with Joey and Nanette years prior for the usual, unfortunate reasons. The Abbots didn't like that Grandmother still kept contact with Joey and Nanette (much to Nanette's displeasure), but because Norma was the chief player that led to everybody's unasked for existence, they let her slide.

Joey dialed up Grandmother while Rich dressed, donning his working gloves and fussing about in the closet garden until it was time to prep for the children. Grandmother Abbot was a reliable soul—there weren't any secrets hiding behind that wrinkled face. Her enthusiasm and general energy sometimes made Joey wonder if she wasn't actually twenty-six puppies in a coat and sun hut. Though Joey knew that Nanette wouldn't do anything drastic, the loss of something vital to her routine was enough to alert the cavalry.

"Joseph?" he heard on the other end. "Oh, lovely! Calling to say hello? Has Nanette got into the trash cans again?"

"Hey, Gran," he chuckled even though her joke was

rather close to reality. "Yeah, just saying hi."

"How's Richard doing?"

"He's good, he's good." Joey glanced over to Rich and watched him mess about with the supply. Rich had this habit of doodling in the soil and leaving Joey hidden notes from time to time.

"You two find time to get away, right? Working with kids, let me tell you, it'll suck the life right out of you. You know you need time. A hobby, a vacation."

"We do, Gran, we do. We like to, uh, garden together."

"Oh lovely… I know you don't like me asking but—"

"Gran—"

"It's my nature, you know. I just want to know—"

"When I know you'll know—"

"—if there was going to be a wedding anytime soon. I'm old. I don't want to wait any longer. If you want, I'll throw a fit like one of those kids of yours and then maybe you'll listen. It's funny really, three grown adults in a house full of children and not a wedding ring between you. Unorthodox, that's what that is." When Norma originally got the news that there were quintuplets in her family, she was ecstatic. Finally she could have the big family she'd always wanted. With the quintuplets, though, two were delinquents, two were milquetoasts, and one ran away to study gospel music. That really only left Joey to help her continue building the Abbot empire. "Which reminds me, how is Nanette?"

"Gran…"

She investigated the tone of his voice right then. "Oh, this is why you've called."

"And to say hi."

"I love you and your cousin very much but sometimes it's lovely just for a chat."

"We are having a chat."

"Yes, I suppose so. What's the problem now? She heckling the toddlers?"

"No, not since we advised her to do it behind their backs. You see, she lost her lunchbox a couple days ago…" The soundless eerie of the other end of the line made Joey question his grandmother's well-being. "Gran? You still there?"

"She lost her lunchbox?"

"Yes."

"I'm coming over. You'll see me this evening."

"You can't drive."

"I'll hitch a ride with Mavis."

"They revoked her license."

"Yes, but not her car. Goodbye. Love you!"

Grandmother Abbot hung up. The phone drifted from Joey's ear as he parroted, "Love you."

And Rich called from across the room, "Love you too."

Wednesdays were when everybody at Baby Badger could feel the week drag on. The boredom of Wednesdays was what would make Thursdays and Fridays so much fun. The Badgers all came back with new ideas to rectify the midweek lull. What Yuki Green loved about this was that Mister Joey would sometimes let them watch Cartoon Network on Wednesdays, which was why Wednesdays were tied for Yuki's favorite day of the week with Monday, Tuesday, Thursday, and Friday.

It was but only noon, and she knew she had to wait longer for Mister Joey to want to turn on the TV. Yuki was in luck because Zola and Virginia had abandoned the blocks so she and the Fieldings could use them.

Some of the best toys in the playroom went to Zola and Virginia first because they knew how to do the coolest things with them. That, and because a lot of the kids felt bad after getting yelled at by Mister Rich because they all laughed when the seven-year-olds hid Virginia's foot during the nap one day. So, the sevens would make up a pretend game to play while Yuki and the Fieldings would try to get some of the good toys to play with. And today was one of those days.

The three kids had all of the big cardboard blocks that were colored red and blue and yellow and green and made to look like a lot of little bricks. Yuki stacked bricks as she listened to Pax. We need to put all the red ones on the bottom because they are the strongest for the whole of the castle. If we mix up the bricks too much it won't look like a castle; it will look like a circus. I think we should mix up the blues and the greens a little bit. It will make the castle look a little cooler. Roux, will you stack this one for me? You have the biggest height. It'll be the best because no monsters will break through the walls.

Yuki was infatuated with something about the Fieldings. From what she could tell they were always so patient with the other, and they hardly ever fought. What two people could go that long without a big fight? It wasn't that the two didn't get on each other's nerves—but the little problems cleared up bloodlessly. Pax and Roux had their own language, it seemed, that an observer could only study but never master.

Yuki's days at the Baby Badger Cub Club were, for the most part, placid.

Roux was quiet. And cool. Roux was the coolest person Yuki knew despite Meadow's arguments. Pax had made her queen of the castle and the two of them were the knights. Roux sat, her legs crossed, on a small bed of yoga mats with her brother off to the side standing guard. The castle was only big enough for the three of them and the slightest amount of space in which to move about. Yuki scampered to the castle wall and scanned out into the kingdom. Out there in the distance, other than Sir Jon who did not fit inside the fort and whose unspoken loyalty to the crown was much appreciated, was a band of travelers from the land of the corner, far beyond the realm of Fielding Field. Yuki listened in on the oddities of the travelers' language:

"Okay, Javy, now you can be Miss Nanette and Meadow and I will try to find you."

The travelers, seven years each, moved about the realm trying to sneak up on one another, trading off which one got to be "Miss Nanette."

Yuki returned to Pax and Roux.

"Have you seen anything weird in the kingdom?" Knight

Pax asked.

"Everything is normal out there," Yuki said, with a bow.

Soon enough, Mister Joey came to collect the kids and bring them up to lunch. Everyone liked Mister Joey just a smidge more than Mister Rich but nobody knew why. Mister Joey was less likely to be sassed or disobeyed, maybe because it was impossible to get a negative reaction out of him. Plus, it was so much fun to have his attention. Even now, Mister Joey walked up to the castle of Fielding Field and picked up both Knight Pax and Yuki and carried them up the stairs to lunch with the queen and the travelers following behind. The kids still liked Mister Rich, but it was like Mister Rich liked Mister Joey in the way that the kids liked Mister Joey. Mister Rich was always pulling him aside and talking about going into the garden.

The garden was a mythical place. It was where the adults disappeared to for minutes, moments, at a time. It was famous among the Badgers, so whenever one of them heard about the garden then for the rest of the day they all would be pulling aside other kids to go there. Nobody knew where the garden was. Most of them thought that it was out in the yard, and though there were some hedges and flowers—mostly dandelions—out there in the yard, it was debatable if any of it all was actually the garden. So, the kids were left with the most effective tool there was in the search for answers: their imaginations. The garden was a fortress, or a palace, a promised land, a farm, a different world; it's where people went when they thought the kids weren't listening. It's where the parents left the responses to questions that they didn't want to answer. Or maybe it was filled with daffodils. It was so easy to forget that that was a possibility.

So, why Mister Rich pulled aside Mister Joey was never answered, only speculated. All the Badgers knew for sure was somewhere there was a garden, and it had all the answers.

Joey and Rich were just sending off the Fieldings when

Nanette rumbled into the garage. Those were the last of the children that needed to be picked up for the day. For the majority, it had been a nice day: sunny, though humid, warm, but with a nice breeze. As it wore on, the sky collected more and more clouds, gradually graying over the palette of oranges and blues. As the garage door shuddered to a close behind Nanette, the first droplets were collecting on the living room window where Joey could see the car carrying Norma Abbot come up the drive.

The car stopped short at a turtle crossing the road, waited for the turtle to move, but when the car figured it would take too long it just overtook the creature and drove onto the property. Joey entered the kitchen just as Nanette did. The oncoming reality of events occurred to Joey: though likely his imagination, he swore he could hear both Nanette's footsteps coming up from the garage and Grandmother's footsteps coming up the front stoop.

When Nanette and Joey saw each other, they nodded.

When the doorbell rang, she asked, "Are there still parents coming by?"

"N-no," he stammered. "Uh, no."

"You are not expecting a delivery, are you?"

"No."

"Well good. It is always nice to finish out the long working day with some of your unannounced friends. Shall I call in a pizza?"

Then Grandmother's voice carried up the stairs, "Thank you, Richard. It really is good to see you. You should call more."

Nanette's glare nearly punched Joey across the face. Anticipating the next move, Joey jumped between Nanette and her escape to the garage.

"Sold out by my own flesh and blood," Nanette sneered.

"She's not the devil, Netty."

"I know that, the devil wishes he could be as persuasive."

"Hello, Nanette," Grandmother said having materialized in the kitchen with Rich to her side. Much like most in the

Abbot house, her smile was indisputable. Nanette scowled enough for everyone. Norma Abbot used to bear most of the qualities of a nursery rhyme teapot, short and stout, but in her later years the stoutness had enervated to more of twiggy frame. Often, the first thing people notice of her was her pair of glasses: the lenses were as thick as her eyesight was unreliable, though she couldn't see well, she noticed everything. Grandmother spoke, "How good to see you."

"Grandmother. How standard to see you."

Rich was the only one in the room who wasn't able to see that Nanette had started to sweat. If she kept it up like this, the pits of her were destined to be the next Niagara Falls. Every few seconds or so Joey noticed Nanette eying the doorknob.

Grandmother was holding a Tupperware container filled with cupcakes. Rich accepted the gift from her and set it down on one of the countertops. It was the only movement in the room for a pregnant seventy-six seconds. Everyone watched as Rich crossed the linoleum tiled floor and slid the container up against the wall, only to then discover his slight discomfort with the realization that he was being scrutinized.

Nanette didn't want to speak first. Joey, it was soon enough clear, wasn't the focus of this conversation. And Grandmother had the composure that said she would happily wait until time came to an end before she uttered the next word. At the same time, Grandmother had the elegance that felt like she was not hurrying anyone to speak. In the end, Nanette groaned aloud (even though she believed that she had kept it in her head).

"What brings you up to the fifth circle today, Grandmother?" she asked.

"A little birdie told me that you were having an issue."

"Yes, well, it's unfortunate that you are so delusional in thinking that birds of any persuasion can talk."

"Yes, a shame."

Rich swallowed. He pondered how a family like this could have produced someone like Joey Abbot.

"We'll let you two talk," Joey said, waving Rich over to

him while he reached for the door.

"You do not have to—"

"Really, Netty, it's no trouble."

And the women were alone.

Nanette wondered about escape. She thought about the delicious appeal of the doorknob, its shimmering beacon leading her to a swift getaway. But the tendrils of Grandmother Abbot, intangible and tenacious, held her put.

It was tough to say how the rift between them originated. Grandmother had always loved Nanette like she had all her grandchildren, and still did. It was within Nanette that the difficulties lay—even though that might come as a shock to some people. Looking at them now it was hard to tell they were related. A sharp eye would notice that the cheekbones were the same, and that if Grandmother's hair hadn't turned gray it'd be the same color as her granddaughter's. But Nanette was much taller, much spindlier. Almost as if she was made of wire. And Grandmother was more so made of kindling—fiery and earthy, built closer to the ground, and flammable.

Norma Abbot, following the mysterious passing of her husband, Horatio, became the first family matriarch in America. Where other powerful women of the Abbot clan either died or left or, in mixing the two together, faking their death, Norma had persisted. Born Norma Pioppo, she was the first of all the Pioppo women to not marry a fully-fledged Italian. Horatio Abbot was only half-Italian, with his mother— to the dissuasions of *la famiglia*—married a lily-white Anglo-Saxon, thus sullying the Italian genes and finally making the family a truly American experience. Though she chalked it up to her Italian blood, Norma's greatest aspiration was to have a comically huge family. She and Horatio had three proud boys to carry on the Abbot name. Unfortunately, the three boys didn't understand how to fulfill their mother's dream. Two of which only had a single child. The third of the Abbot boys knew what his mother wanted and had five kids at once. This made Norma positively giddy until about four years after the quintuplets' birth when the kids turned out to be, more or less, pieces of, well, you know. But she loved them anyway.

Nowadays, Grandmother could be found gallivanting about town with red-hatted women, all with some new novel in their right hands and theatre tickets in their left. Now that she had time and money and family that was more or less negligent of her, she spent most of her days doing what she thought was living: bus rides to Foxwoods and trips to exotic lands, like Northern Ireland. Or the Everglades. She always wanted to wrestle a crocodile, but since her knees went bunk she's had to settle for helping raise Nanette.

Though it wasn't couth of her to pick favorites among her grandchildren, she decided to be vague about her preferences. She could confidently state that Nanette and Joey were on the same end of the spectrum. Her jaunts about the world made her children jealous, as they were all married to suburban New England lives. Her adventures let her captivate her sons and their wives and select members of their children to the point that she could nonchalantly ask for help moving house or making dinner and have them all agree without realizing it first.

Despite her better judgment, Nanette found her grandmother's hold on the family to be tenuous at best. Grandmother, for Nanette's entire life, had been putting together fruitless attempts to indoctrinate Nanette with friendship. Whether or not Grandmother wanted Nanette to accept her as a friend, she believed that it was important for Nanette to have at least one. Thankfully, Joey took it on effortlessly. Even if Nanette didn't understand that she was friends with her cousin, at least Grandmother could see it.

"I brought you cupcakes," Grandmother chirped.

"So you have."

Grandmother crossed over to a spare glass that had been left on the counter. Using her thin, thin fingers she twisted it around in place as she spoke to her granddaughter.

"I heard you have a little problem."

"You have mentioned that already."

"Ha, silly me. I remember now."

Delusional old bitty, Nanette thought but didn't say because it was too rude, "You hen."

"Rudeness. That's why you have so few friends, Nanette."

"That is where you are wrong, Grandmother. I do not have friends. So there."

"Give yourself some credit."

"All your past shenanigans to inculcate me into some social group have all failed gloriously and I can proudly say that I am in charge of my life now."

"I never claimed to be in charge of you, Nanette. I just want to help you like I want to help all my grandkids."

"Even Mo?"

"Well Mo's a special case."

"I am sure."

Grandmother picked the glass up off the counter and held it up to the light. After, she used her cardigan to rub out an invisible smudge.

"I'll be staying in the area for a couple days. Maybe the week."

"It is a shame that we haven't the space."

"No worries, love, I'll be staying with Mavis and her kids tonight. Then I'm making rounds to see the rest of the family. But I'll be nearby. I might come back in a couple days."

"I do love a good omen."

"For someone who thinks herself the height of morality, and the standard for expectation, you seem to forget who you are talking to. I am your grandmother and I love you. It's in your best interest to remember that. Your best interest."

Grandmother stopped cleaning the glass. She walked toward the exit, stopping just short of the door. "And Nanette ..."

"Yes, Grandmother?"

"I'll keep an eye out for your lunchbox. Losing it. That's unlike you." She then left, intentionally leaving out a goodbye.

Nanette was left alone. It took her a few moments to recognize that her legs were quaking. She scanned the room, trying to anchor herself again. Her focus landing on the glass that Grandmother was polishing. Nanette hobbled over to the glass and examined it.

Spotless.

Immaculate.

Perfect.

Without another thought, Nanette charged over to the trash can and threw the glass out. She reveled in the crisp, cacophonous shattering of the glassware against the bottom of the bin. It gave her next to no relief as she bent over the can, feeling her lungs constrict and release faster, sharper than was normal.

She listened to her Grandmother's words play over and over in her head. *You seem to forget who you're talking to… It's in your best interest…* She also remembered I brought you cupcakes but that one was secondary to her overall fright.

If Norma Abbot thought that she could pop in to Nanette's home and threaten her, well … then Nanette would just have to do something about that. For years now, Grandmother had loomed over Nanette. Glowering, the old woman's presence, *nay*, her mere mention was a constant threat to Nanette. At any point, the work she had spent building her little world, her home, her little clan, it could all implode in on her—leaving her in an empty space without even a lunchbox to comfort her. And, oh, that sweet veneer of Grandmother Abbot had them fooled. It took a human chisel like Nanette to see through all of that. To chip away. Nanette didn't believe in destiny, however she did believe in self-assurance. And if one of them was anything like the other, then it was their destiny for one of them to make a martyr of the other.

Nanette Abbot had but one major secret in this life. And it was hardly a secret at all, hardly worth mentioning. But she refused adamantly of its coming to public knowledge. Not for any real important reason because of, because of—who really knew why? Nanette batted the thought around in her head for a couple minutes before writing off the possibility of this.

If she had only one major secret, she'd preferably keep it that way

CHAPTER FIVE

YUKI GREEN

When Nanette pulled onto her street after work the next day, she failed to notice that her knee wouldn't stop bouncing. She had a restless night, a bag lunch, and a spreadsheet with only one point of data filled in on it. She couldn't let Grandmother beat her to her own lunchbox just on principle. Nanette didn't need her Grandmother's help, just as Grandmother didn't need any more borrowed time.

As she drove along the lane, she saw a familiar, unfamiliar car pulling out of her driveway. Nanette's grasp tightened on her steering wheel as she passed right by her house.

Tsukuru Green changed his last name coming into the country to help him make it as an American businessman. His wife, Betty Green, being a second generation and full-blooded Japanese woman, enjoyed that Tsukuru was fluent in the language that she had never actually learned. Mister Green ended up as a corporate translator for Honda, and, on the side, he freelanced transcribing young adult novels from English. He wanted to translate novels both to and from Japanese but he was upset with the few books on American shelves that came in from overseas.

Tsukuru was a charmer. He'd beguiled his wife's parents, grandparents, and most of his cohorts over at Honda. He found humor in the western work ethic, how it was so expected to hate one's job, or at least aspects of it. People vied for the weekends, when they stepped away in order to forget how they spend their weekdays. As he went through his days, jocular and jovial, his coworkers had patted him on the back, and his in-laws said sweet things about him on Facebook, and then he'd get home and instantaneously commence shouting at his wife.

Tsukuru and Betty got their exercise through argument. They were so religiously litigious that they soundproofed specific rooms of their modest suburban home to keep the neighbors from phoning up the police anymore. Even now, as Tsukuru adjusted his rearview mirror to check up on little Yuki in her car seat, he was running through all the things he could possibly shout about when he pulled into his own garage. After his work, his wife, and his daughter, Tsukuru's favorite thing was to make a scene in the sanctity of his home.

When they arrived home, Betty was waiting for the groceries to be delivered. She wanted to put Yuki to bed before then so she wouldn't have to worry about juggling the delivery, the daughter, and the husband. But as usual, Tsukuru was using up all the time he needed. Betty wasn't too hard on Tsukuru, though, when he was coming home from Baby Badger because she knew that Joey and Rich had taken him in for a few minutes and fixed him up with a snack before sending him along on his way.

Betty liked those boys. She had met Joey a few years ago when he walked into her barbershop for an emergency haircut. Joey had liked the job Betty had done so much he just kept making the trip back to her, and eventually they got to talking about who-did-what for a living. It was Betty's dream to, one day, have her own hair styling studio and she believed that the dream was wholly achievable at this point in time. If Tsukuru quit dragging himself to let her invest then they wouldn't even need to argue about it. But Betty liked the challenge, the immutable thrill of the fight for what she wanted. And Tsukuru, for all his blessings, looks, charms, and knacks, he was a fight. Betty Green didn't know how those boys got on as they did—she never saw them arguing, not even in the suppressed subtextual way one may witness while they picked up their kid. She was sure it happened, but she supposed it was more of a statement depending on the couple—

"There you are. You know the groceries will be here soon and you just want me to bring them all in by myself!" Betty yelled this all from the upstairs window as she saw her husband's car park.

Tsukuru undid the fasteners on the car seat, listening to the muffled banshee cries that were pushing through the walls of the house. He picked up the little girl and asked her if she was excited to be home after a fun day with her friends. Yuki nodded and then watched her shouting mother in the window. When they got inside, the mother's berating taunts persisted and all that came out of the husband's mouth was "Wait" every couple seconds or so.

Wait. Wait. Wait.

He took Yuki into her bedroom and set her down on the bed. He kissed her on the forehead in his usual, reserved way.

"Okay," he said, and then to his wife, *"How was I to know that the groceries were coming today? It's not every day we order our groceries—"* He closed up the nursery behind him.

Yuki watched the voices through the wall. It was impossible to tell what all the yelling was about, but it didn't frighten her because it was all that she knew. The days were soft, the nights were loud, and that was life.

When the three of them did things together it was always civil. On special nights, her mom read her Goodnight Moon and then her dad would translate it into Japanese and they'd banter on whose was better. Yuki didn't know a lot of Japanese, but from how her father made it sound, she knew more than her mother. The verbal ballistics thundered outside of Yuki's little bedroom door. It made it impossible to hear a particular frenzied car driving by.

"She's late," Rich said, drying off a plate and returning it to the cabinet.

"I guess she is," Joey said as he rinsed the dishes in the sink.

"And you're not worried?"

"She's constantly reminding us that she's a big girl. If it was Al or Callie we wouldn't be thinking twice about it."

"Our friends aren't your cousin. She's made that clear."

"Come on now, Rich. If Nanette didn't like us then she wouldn't let us live here, work here."

Joey handed Rich another plate. Rich passively set it down on the countertop without drying it off first. He threw his washcloth over his shoulder and stared up at the ceiling. Joey glancing over at him, grabbed the plate, and dried it off himself.

"Well I'm worried," Rich said. "One thing goes wrong in years and all of a sudden it feels like she's collapsing. What if she goes through our things again?"

"We're home all the time. At least when she's here. She wouldn't have the chance to find anything before one of us could stop her."

"I'm worried, Joey."

"Hey, hey."

Joey put down the dish he was scrubbing and shut off the faucet. He pulled Rich to his chest and played with his hair. "This'll blow over. Nanette will be back to her normal self."

"It's not just about Nanette."

"Why, what's up?"

"We're hardworking, right? We make 'decent' money. Much better than most people our age. What are we still doing here? Why do I have to fear your cousin exploding every single minute I see her and every single second I don't? Let's leave, Joey. Let's move to a new house. A smaller one, just big enough for all the kids and us and maybe even a little garden. A real garden."

"That's a pretty big commitment."

"Yeah, well."

Rich placed his head against Joey's chest and felt it expand with a large breath. He felt a slow kiss on his forehead, forcing himself to relax into the embrace.

The boys thought separately: they did have the means, the enterprise. Rich's father, before they fell out of favor, was always exhausting the old phrase: you got to pick yourself up by your bootstraps. He'd loved that phrase even though Rich's father was born into old money; Rich Eliot learned a while ago that his father's wealth was able to convince him of a lot of things. Rich didn't see any of that money, and he definitely got none of the support. If anything, Rich was trying to find his own bootstraps—if he could find them then maybe he could pick them up.

Rich wanted to move on from all of his family. Not just Nanette.

Or maybe he wanted his family the way it used to be. He wasn't sure. It was a hopeless ideal, putting his family back together. He resented them all for loving him unconditionally for his entire life and then, having found their condition, leaving. He was afraid of this newfound need for vindication, but he kept himself from suppressing its persuasive charms Rich would find himself making up conversations of his future success and the family needing him and then him turning his back. Conversations of him regaining his power. Conversations of his father realizing just how much of his son Rich really was. And he couldn't get there by living in his boyfriend's cousin's basement.

Joey, it must be said, understood this. However, for all of his cousin's intricacies she had never truly wronged him. She was reluctant to welcome him back into the house simply because she unquestioningly enjoyed her solitude, not from any familial pressure to turn her back to them. Joey did wonder on occasion if Nanette had spite for these circumstances, but at the same time he was her only connection to the rest of the family. Even Nanette's parents went to Joey for updates on their daughter.

Sure, it was likely that Nanette wanted them in the house.

And it was likely that she was even okay with them staying in the house. But perhaps it was finally time to consider the big move. Across town, maybe, to stay close and to keep it so the parents wouldn't need to find a new daycare for the kids, even though that felt somewhat like a secondary reason to the fact that the parents would need to find a new person that would sell them pot.

And that was another thing, he thought. *What if they had a real garden, with perennials and shit?* Joey always thought about how they don't smoke anymore. And, frankly, he figured that it was probably unsettling for the parents to leave their kids here with the knowledge that they were casual dealers regardless of the fact that all the parents partook themselves. Thankfully it hadn't been much of a problem so far.

All the same, a house. People Joey's age didn't get houses; they got sad.

Devil magic was needed to whip up a dual-income household with thousands in savings ready to be bled. Plus, houses really were for families. Joey remembered the heavy silence of this home when he first moved in with Nanette back at the end of his undergraduate years. Chillingly quiet, all he could hear were the spectral steps of Nanette's morning routine. He wished he knew how she could live like that.

"We can think about it," Joey said.

"Only think about it?"

"We can talk about it, too."

"That's it?"

"It'll take some time."

"No way, buster. If we want to leave we can be gone in no time. Trust me," Rich said. "Do you trust me?"

"I trust you."

"No, do you trust me?"

Joey laughed. "Well, now you got me questioning it."

Rich ultimately acquiesced, "Fine, we can think about it and come back."

Already he was thinking about the places they could stay on short notice and imagining a real estate agent coming in and figuring out all their wants and needs. He compiled all his materials for an argument, should there end up being one. But for now, he was content with think about it and come back.

"Still," Rich said, "I am worried about Nanette. There's no telling what she could be up to."

Nanette had never seen this neighborhood. It was a lot like her own. Suburban, filled with new families, and it was very easy to hear somebody complaining about having to mow their grass. If she wasn't so averse to the idea of making idle chatter with strangers, she might've taken a walk along this road.

She parked up the street, under the overarching canopy of an oak tree. The feigning sunlight cast saffron shadows onto the pavement. The soft lilt of a breeze carried Nanette along the road until she stopped at the target house. A nice split-level, it looked near identical to Nanette's own abode. There was a modest stoop leading to the front door and the purity of the white siding was emphasized by the verdant expanse of the lawn. Nanette heard muffled cries and exasperations coming through from the upper floor and was consequently reminded of her younger days spent with Grandmother. Suppressing a nostalgic flare, Nanette stepped onto the grass.

If this house was anything like her own, then the kitchen would be toward the back of the house on the top floor. Scooting across the lawn, she darted into the backyard in hopes of finding some ingress. What she found was a dark teak staircase leading up to a deck with a round patio table and a couple chairs beside a propane barbecue grill. *Tritely Americana,* Nanette thought as she ascended.

Nearing the top, the ululations from within grew even more intense. *I didn't know it was grocery day now did I? I was busy picking up our daughter from that den! Oh, so it's my fault that you're a forgetful husband? I do all the housework just so you can take your time? That is not fair! You're always saying things aren't fair. Maybe fair doesn't exist. Maybe we just make our own rules in this house. That is exactly what we do, we are the parents.* The rapidity with which the dispute occurred made it difficult for Nanette to differentiate who was in fact talking.

When she made it to the top of the steps, she found a glass sliding door leading into the house. The door was closed, so Nanette just leered through the glass displaying as little of herself as she possibly could. The door connected to a dining room that was connected to the kitchen, just like in her home. But unlike her home, there was no partition between the dining room and the living room where the screaming parents were yelling at each other.

From their appearances, Nanette reckoned she knew which of the children that this house belonged to: she couldn't recall a specific name, but she knew the child as "girl." It was as descriptive as Nanette could be seeing that she had no reputable qualities of her own other than her friendship to other children at Baby Badger. She wasn't quiet enough to be the quiet one, nor was she obnoxious enough to be memorable.

Standing there, Nanette decided she needed to formulate a plan. One hadn't been necessary seeing how just winging it had gotten her this far. Nanette conspired that if she knocked on the front door and then ran back here then that might give her the leeway to enter the home. If she could run back in forty-five seconds and it took them at least a minute to answer the door then that would give her at least fifteen seconds to get in, search the kitchen completely, and get out. *I've done more with less*, she thought.

Before she set out down the stairs, the doorbell rang.

"*It's the groceries*," the woman yelled.

"*I'll help you with those*," the man replied.

Addicted to the result, Nanette watched as the two adults left the room. Sure that the upper floor was vacant, Nanette slid inside. The conditioned air hit her in the face as she pulled the door closed behind her. It would've been rude to leave the door open and let all of that air out of the house.

She went to the refrigerator, as was custom, and checked the spot where she usually keeps her lunchbox. But it wasn't in there. The inside had shelves in a different, much less efficient configuration than her own refrigerator. The lack of lunchtime foods gave Nanette the impression that these savages purchased their lunches every day. If the lunchbox was here then it must be collecting dust in one of the cabinets. She calculated the approximate time she had left by the sound of rustling plastic bags and relatively civil bickering coming back up the stairs.

Nanette began opening and closing as many cabinets as she could, investigating faster than light could travel. At least it felt that way. After making it through the whole kitchen when she heard a most distressing sound.

"Miss Nanette?"

She turned to find little Yuki Green standing in the archway of the kitchen. The girl was on edge, wondering what arcane horrors could summon Miss Nanette to her home.

"Oh, for heaven's sake. You can walk?" Nanette rushed over to the child and picked her up. Yuki did happen to be small for her age, but Nanette was surprised that any of the children under five had any sense of mobility. She tried her best to keep the girl as far away from her body as possible. "Which is your room?"

"That one."

"Alright."

Nanette wanted to make a break for the girl's room. Hopefully she could write it off as a hallucination or a game or *whatever* and the girl would forget all about it. After all she was only … what, a couple months old? A year, if that? She didn't think they started remembering things until they were at least four.

Yuki, who was four, was busy remembering everything.

"How did you find me?" Nanette questioned.

"It was quiet."

"Oh yeah?"

"Quiet can be a good thing. I like quiet."

"You are wrong, but, granted, you are a fetus, so I'll let it slide." Nanette considered her opportunity for the investigation. "Okay, where is it?"

"What?" the child replied.

"We can all play coy if we want to, but I'll tell you it will go much easier if you just tell me where it is."

"What is it?" The pitch in her voice was rising and she wouldn't meet Nanette's eyes.

"The lunchbox. Tell me where you hid the lunchbox."

"What?"

Nanette's eye twitched, meaning that she could begrudgingly mark this child as innocent. With the inquisition complete, she was prepared to warn the girl that she saw nothing today.

"Who are you?" harked a voice.

Nanette spun around to find Betty and Tsukuru Green standing down the hallway with their arms loaded with plastic grocery bags.

"Why do you have our daughter?" Betty continued.

"I'll call the police," Tsukuru said.

"No!" Nanette yelped. "No police. And no worries. I understand how this might look like a sticky situation of sorts but rest assured I in no way mean any harm."

"What's your name?" Tsukuru barked.

"Ahhhhhhhhhhhhhh… nette. Annette." Nanette cheered internally, feeling as if she totally nailed it. "My name is understandably Annette and I was just on my way out."

"Why did you make your way in?" Betty sneered.

"Because I am with . . . grocery store chain and we want to know how your delivery experience has been. On a scale of 'adequate' to 'could be more adequate,' would you say you'd shop with us again?"

The Greens lowered their shopping bags to the carpet as one said, "Adequate," and the other, "Could be more adequate."

Nanette put Yuki down, who then sprinted (well, she was young so it was more of a speed-wobble) into her bedroom and slammed the door behind her. She enjoyed the peaceful seconds with Miss Nanette more than she thought she could but she knew that the way her parents looked at each other meant…

What do you mean you had an adequate experience? You have census workers invading our home! They just want to be thorough, you wouldn't know anything about thoroughness because you struggle with execution. Oh, I'll show you an execution. Go ahead—MAKE MY DAY.

Panicked, Nanette approached the feud. "Whoa, whoa, whoa, whoa. Let us all calm down, Mister and Misses …. Child-haver."

Tsukuru said, "It's Green."

But Nanette, who was too scared to pay full attention, said, "I'm sure it'll clear up. Listen, we at the . . . the grocery store hate to see, uh, hostility between our—shall we say—devoted customers. I feel like it is my duty to ask just, just, just how we can make your day just a little … softer."

"Are you qualified to help with this sort of thing?"

"Well, um, that is a smidgen of a gray area. What I can do for sure is send you a voucher for, uh, beans."

"But that's all?" Betty sighed.

"If there is anything you wish to talk about, let me know. If not, I will get out of your absolutely divine home and never return. Never. And I am a grocery … census taker of my word, let me tell you."

Nanette inched toward the stairs to the front door.

"Okay," said Tsukuru.

"What?" the women replied, agape.

"I want my day to be a little softer."

Betty stepped between Tsukuru and Nanette, "Forgive my husband. His English is a little … you know." This was obviously a lie on Betty's part, as one could argue that Tsukuru's English was the better out of the two.

"Every day," Tsukuru continued, "it's yell and shout at this and shout and yell at that and I thought I liked it. I used to like it—but we're older now, Betty. We have a daughter to look out for. Who knows what creeps will come along in her lifetime? Is this shouting and yelling world really what's best for our family? We soundproofed our kitchen. Our kitchen. The neighbors must think we're serial killers."

"Isn't that just someth—" Nanette was cut off.

"My voice has gotten so much more gravelly than it had been when we met," Tsukuru went on. "We used to sing together, remember? I don't even think my voice could handle that now."

"Oh, Tsukuru," Betty said, glossy-eyed.

"Oh, Seppuku," Nanette unwittingly parroted.

"And sure, I haven't been the best husband but I can get better. We can sit down together and chat. We could debate if you still want a challenge. I know how you like to challenge yourself."

"I do," Betty said and smiled. "I would like that. As long as we still did something together, Tsu. It doesn't have to be yelling."

"No, it does not," Nanette threw in.

"Or debating, or singing," Betty said. "My friends like to garden with each other. What if we gardened?"

"That sounds nice," Tsukuru replied. "We wouldn't have to grow what they do, though, right?"

"No, we'll find what we like."

The Greens flew into each other's arms and held it just long enough for Nanette to want to leave. The couple said nothing. Ignoring Nanette's presence completely, they breathed synchronously.

Nanette began down the stairs. "Tha—" she stammered, "Thanks for shopping at the grocery store."

On her way out, she passed a man with a backwards cap and a clipboard. "I need someone to sign for the groceries," he said.

But Nanette ignored him. She fast-walked up the road and found her car parked under the oaken canopy. As she turned off the street, she recollected what that little girl said to her. Quiet can be a good thing. Nanette nearly laughed. She was so small, with so much to figure out about the world.

CHAPTER SIX

THE ELIOT FAMILY TRUST

Around 7:00 p.m. Thursday, the work that Rich and Joey would generally be doing at the desk in their bedroom took place on the counters in the kitchen. Joey sat atop the counter, breathing steadily but clicking the button of his pen over and over and over and over until Rich hoped the spring would wear out.

They'd updated their files. They had a planner that told them which kids would be in Baby Badger and when—like next week it was looking that Figgy would only be in for three days rather than the usual five. Though Joey liked having Figgy around, it came down to what the parents needed. After all, that's how Baby Badger started: just Joey and Rich doing their part to help the parents relax.

Joey stared at the door to the garage, waiting. Rich was the opposite, looking everywhere except that door. The further the clock ticked from 6:30, the less comfortable the guys became. It wasn't even late; it was just late for a certain somebody. She could've been mugged, or kidnapped, or rather if she was kidnapped they'd likely have returned her by now. But she could easily have been robbed.

The end-of-day cleanup was complete, and now all the

guys had were their imaginations to harass them. For all their disparities, there was one major similarity between these two Abbot cousins: they didn't care to use their imaginations for anything. Both Joey and Nanette liked to know the whole reality of any given situation. To put it simply: if there was a blank, they didn't want to fill it in. One of the reasons Joey loved working with kids so much was that they did so much imagining for him and he just had to go along with it. Nanette, rather, was averse to the whole construction of fantastical realms. She just didn't get it. And then there was Rich, who was entirely separate from the Abbot blood and let his imaginations dance around his head.

Some said that Rich's imaginative affliction was the result of him having ambition. Not that the Abbots lacked ambition. In fact, Nanette had for the most part efficiently achieved all her ambitions by the age of thirty, although since then she had stabilized her wants and hadn't reached for anything more. Joey didn't exactly have as much ambition as he had luck: pleasantly falling into a fulfilling position that he could see himself doing indefinitely. But Rich wanted more. He loved the kids but he dreamed of a daycare that wasn't just his house. He wanted his own yard for his own kids someday. He wanted a husband who would help him build a family. He wanted to say goodbye to Nanette and finally move on from her and her anal proclivities. He wanted, he wanted, he wanted.

Oddly enough, now he wanted Nanette to be home.

Not—most likely—out of any sentimentality for Nanette's safety, but more because he wanted to not worry about her unhinging. Much like Joey, he was worried that Nanette was about to do something regretfully stupid.

"Can you believe this?" Rich said.

"I know," Joey replied.

"Half an hour."

"I know."

Joey, not to minimize Rich's emotions, liked when he saw Rich get worried. At least when it came to family issues. Over the years, Rich had become desensitized to the goings-on of both his and Joey's families. Not that it was of any surprise to Joey. He and Rich had faced similar losses since the happy and frivolous days of college. Rich just lost a bit more in regards to some security he'd been promised throughout his life. It was one of the reasons he abhorred things that went awry.

Rich's great-grandfather founded the Eliot Paper Factory which supplied all New England with its stationary needs, branching out with locations beyond Boston near Philadelphia and Schenectady. When his great-grandfather retired, the next generation of Eliots was trusted to take over. This expectation only lasted through to the second generation though, as Rich's father needed to be threatened into keeping charge of the business in order to keep the money in the family. Rich's father became a resentful man, stuck in his father's job of literally pushing paper. Rich never felt bad for his father though on account of his father having no other prospects—Old Mister Eliot was loathe to the business because he spent his entire childhood without real responsibility, but since he was the oldest he'd been shoved into the position while his somehow more negligible siblings pursued their fancies on the factory's expense. Perhaps if his father wanted to do something else with his life—be a doctor or an artist or something else of passion and consequence—Rich would mourn his father's soul. However, the supposed totalitarian control of his wife and children that Old Mister Eliot assumed as his only true modicum of strength, will, and power made it so that he was only unabashedly personable when tipsy.

So when Rich opened up to his father about his identity, his love for the foolish Joseph Abbot, he was shunned. Disowned wouldn't be the word for it because Rich's siblings tried to keep in touch. Rarely, but enough, and with little success. And seeing how nobody was willing to stand against Old Mister Eliot, for fear of their own expulsion from the wealth and Eliot name, they all opted for the side of Rich's father.

He cried until he was numb. And then he didn't cry again.

Now, Rich manifested familial grief by working, by pacing

the length of the kitchen, by tossing around in his sleep, and whenever that similar stress shimmered out of the shadows he would only look at it through the corner of his eye. To stare at it directly would be too easily blinding.

The familiar rumors of Nanette's car pulled into the garage.

Moments later, Nanette entered the kitchen and moved about in her usual post-workday way: putting down her backpack, hanging up her coat, placing her keys in that little dish that Joey got because he thought it was cute even though it was in the spot she used to use for her fruit bowl. Not distractedly, Nanette walked about as if she was zeroed in on something outside of herself. Rich and Joey stared at her until her gait slowed and she turned to the others.

"It's late, Nanette," Rich said.

"Yes," Nanette said. "That is one of the inevitabilities of time. Good night."

"Whoa, hey," Joey said, hopping down from the countertop. "It's not that late."

"It's late for her," Rich stated. And Nanette nodded. "Are you telling me that it's not worth an explanation? Why shouldn't we have reason to freak out? For the first time since forever you're a full half an hour late?"

"I fail to recognize why it is that you feel owed these declarations, Richard," she spat, "It is my house and I should be able to mix up my comings and goings as I please. Somedays I would be a little early, and other days I should spend coming home a little late, and there is nothing that should worry you in the slightest."

"There we go," Joey said.

"No, no," said Rich. "Joey, you can't not wonder where she was? Netty, you've never been late before."

"You are right, Richard," Nanette glared, "I must be demented for having forgotten that after paying the utility bills and stocking the kitchen and providing security for you that I also am the prisoner and you the warden. That I, after all my troubles and most recent distresses, am still bound to you.

Obliged to will away the hours until I can return to my cell and listen to you and your Number One over there mooning and swooning and waiting for my subordination."

"You're exaggerating!"

"If I have told you once then I have told you a million times that I do not exaggerate."

"You don't think—like, it honestly doesn't occur to you—that something like this might worry us? What if you came back in the middle of the night and Joey might dropkick you because he thought you were a burglar or something?"

"Immediately your analogy makes no sense. I would be able to best Joey in a fight. Easily."

"Hey," Joey disagreed.

"Though he may have me beat in stature, he entirely lacks technique."

"Nanette!" Rich yelled, "That's not the point and you know it. Why can't we just talk civilly?!"

"*You want to talk civilly?*"

"*Yes! It would be my dream to talk civilly!*"

Though noticed only by Joey, the volume increased harshly every time someone shouted civilly. He wanted to interject, but he didn't think his voice went this loud.

"*Well then, may the civility commence!*" Slamming about, Nanette pulled a kettle out of the cabinet and prepared tea. "Chamomile or Earl flipping Grey?"

"Nanette—" Joey couldn't get a word out.

"Do we have any mint?"

"No! I have to go shopping."

"Chamomile!"

"I thought so."

"Guys, come on—"

They both reprimanded: "Shut up, Joseph!"

Nanette and Rich squabbled about unintelligibly as the tea was made. Occasionally a lucid *civilly* was thrown in but Joey couldn't catch the specifics. When it was ready, Joey must have lost focus for a second because a cup of tea appeared in his hands. Rich and Nanette were holding their respective cups, locked in an unerring bout of eye contact. Neither of them wanted to be the first one to sip.

Silence.

Joey watched the quaint porcelain cups. Rich held his by the handle, steadily, without any indication that he was about to sip, whereas—despite the likely scalding sensation—Nanette held her cup in her palm, unaffected by the unavoidable burn of the surface. Joey blew the steam off his, taking small sips. It occurred to him that tea must have been Nanette's chief idea of civility. However, with the aching seconds of neither of the arguing parties drinking, that assertion might be changing.

Rich's finger finally twitched. Without speaking, he raised his cup, not up to his mouth though. No, he brought the tea over the kitchen sink and poured it down the drain, all the while not breaking Nanette's stare. Nanette followed suit, she lifted her cup but misjudged the distance to the sink and ended up draining her cup right onto the countertop, pooling in a steaming puddle until dribbling onto the floor. Also, all the while, not breaking the eye contact between them.

Slowly, and together, Rich and Nanette set down their cups in the sink to be washed later. They took two deep breaths and smiled.

Civilly, Rich belted, *"You see that mess?! You know who's going to clean that tea off the counter?"*

"I will take care of it just like how I made the tea? Not that you seemed to care or offer a scintilla of gratitude!"

"A scintilla of grati—We do the chores around here!"

"Oh, how could I have forgotten all the cleaning up you do after those goshforsaken children that you bring into my home. While I do everything else."

"You don't do everything around here, you self-centered knob. How dense are you?"

"Is that a rhetorical question?"

"What do you even mean?!"

"I am not dense! I am airy, the epitome of easy-breezy. And if you cannot see that then you might be the dense one."

"You are airy like a hurricane, Nanette! If you were an animal,

you'd be a stampede!"

"Au contraire!"

"*No, no—I will* au contraire."

There was then the sound of the hallway door shutting and Nanette and Rich saw that Joey had left the room. A shared moment of unnerving silence ensued. They listened to the rumble of the air conditioning.

GREAT, Rich thought. Now Joseph was mad at him—but what's worse was that Joseph wasn't even on his side. How could one problem simultaneously be two problems?

"For once," Nanette sneered, "Joey has got the right idea."

She took a step to the door. Rich reached for her elbow but she pulled her arm away too quickly.

"All in the technique," she chided.

"Tell me where you were."

"*Au contraire,*" she said, and left the kitchen.

Rich imploded. He bared his hands down onto one of the countertops. But, having forgotten that Nanette had just spilt scalding tea there, pulled his hands away in pain, yelping. He ripped some paper towels off of the roll and mopped up.

Minutes passed with him drying the same spot of the counter.

In the alleged peace, Rich wondered.

He threw out the wasted towels and sank to the floor, his back pressed against the cabinet door. Pulling his knees closer to him, he whipped out his phone and scrolled through his contacts.

If dust could collect on names in a phone, then Rich thought he needed to brush off his brother's number.

The electric name of Cass Eliot peered through the screen. Rich hadn't sought out his older brother for about two years now. They spoke rarely in that time. Sometimes they would have lunch orchestrated surreptitiously by their younger sister, Dorie. Unfortunately those few lunchtime meetings came to an end as the elder brothers grew wise to her mediatory ways.

Rich never wanted to hate his brother. He didn't know if he could, but on principle Rich felt as if he should. Cass was fast to give him up when it was his father's wish to do so. Cass was likely to take over the paper factory and had all the means to accomplish that. It didn't help that Rich majored in French rather than business like Cass had (though in all fairness, Rich had at least minored in business). But, Rich had a memory so old that he couldn't recall if he had made it up or not: he and Cass wanted to run the paper factory together someday. This was before they learned about their father's soulless career and subsequent decline in amicability. But it may have been destined for the whole family to have a subsequent decline in amicability.

And yet, Rich's thumb hovered over his brother's name. He knew that there wasn't a chance of his brother messaging him first. He would have to put the work in if they were going to be friends. But he also knew that he no longer desired to be friends with his brother. He just wanted to call him up and complain about family troubles as if they were in high school again and Rich was lying about having a girlfriend while Cass was lying about how many girlfriends he had.

Going against his commonsense, Rich pressed down. The screen altered for two reasons: to inform that he was calling Cass Eliot and to terrify him.

"Uh, Rich?" Cass's Southie accent pushed through. Rich only had the accent when he returned home, which he hadn't done for a while. "Rich?"

"Cass."

"Holy shit. Where've you been, Rich? When's the last time…"

"Christmas."

"Wow."

"Last Christmas."

"Time… Why're you callin', Rich?"

"How's the family?"

"The family? Why do you care?"

"It's my family, Cass."

"Yeah, yeah. I know that. We've been, uh, you know. We've been managing."

"How's Ma?"

"Quiet."

"Dorie?"

"Starting at Amherst."

"And Dad?"

"The usual."

"Sorry to hear that."

"He's not that bad, Rich. You should know that by now. He just likes things his own way." Rich read too much into his brother's tone. He couldn't decipher whether his brother felt compelled to defend his father or if he genuinely believed in his father's negotiable charisma. Either way, the inherent words were enough to keep Rich uncomfortable. Would it really be too much for someone to call their father an ass?

"I've spent a lot of time with people who need things a certain way, Cass. They're not as bad as Dad."

"I guess it's just the company then… Okay, cut the crap, Rich. Why'd you call?"

"We weren't friends, were we?"

"Friends? Brothers, Rich. A little different."

"We have a couple pairs of siblings here at the daycare. Best friends."

"Kids."

"We got along, at least. Didn't we?"

"We knew where we stood with Pa."

"A little different."

"Dorie misses you."

"Someone has to."

"Ey, that's not fair. I cared about you and you left. We all did."

"I remember it all a little differently."

"Don't be so dramatic, Rich. Damn it."

"Dorie misses me?"

"Yeah. Her birthday's next week."

"I know."

"We're throwin' a party. She'd probably like to see you. It's a surprise party."

"Would Dad be there?"

"Yeah. You know, you could make amends with him. Try."

"Why's that my responsibility?"

"Because Pa doesn't give two shits about your feelings. But if you showed up, maybe brought a date, who knows? Might make him smile."

Cass never needed to worry about bringing a date to show off at family gatherings anymore ever since he married a girl that—as everyone anticipated—was too good for him. Rich saw the humor of his brother's shotgun wedding and how it felt like Rich would never have that problem to preoccupy him. But as long as they were happy, Rich supposed, that was what mattered. It was all that he was after, too.

"A date? When is this?"

"This Sunday. At my place because it's a surprise party."

"This Sunday… I don't know if Joe…"

"No, not Joe, Rich. A girl. Bring a girl. A guy isn't gonna make amends with Pa. Think for once."

"I thought when you said try…"

"If it's not a girl, you're better off staying wherever it is you are these days."

"Right."

"Right."

"Goodbye, Cass."

"Wait, wait. Tell me why you called."

"I was hoping to find someone less stubborn."

"Less stubborn than who?"

"It doesn't matter. Bye Cass. It was nice talking."

"Yeah. Uh, if you're serious about seeing Dorie, uh, it's the same address. The Medford house. We'll be movin' soon." This was somewhat startling to Rich because his brother moved to the Medford house shortly after he got married and bragged about how it was literally the greatest house for a guy like him. With something as big as moving house, Rich pondered how much of the old life kept trudging on without him.

"Thanks, Cass."

"Bye, Rich."

"Bye, Cass."

Rich sat alone on the kitchen floor. He was in the darkness—the sun had gone down since the yelling spree with Nanette. With his phone off and his voice on hiatus he saw how abysmal the room was.

Nothing had changed on his brother's end. He should've called Dorie but there wouldn't have been anything she could do. And he was fairly certain his mom didn't have her own phone. Not her own decision—it was just that Old Mister Eliot thought that she would be fine using the house phone. Rich had learned that if he ever returned to his life with the Eliot family, it would mean lying, copiously. He had to compromise all the work he had done actualizing himself just to suffice the comfort of his family. This was their love's condition, he thought. He was the aberration of the lineage. He was as headstrong as his father, as forward-thinking, as industrious. He shouldn't have to fear his father. Rather, he shouldn't have had to fear his father. The terror was done. The bogeyman of past efforts shaped Rich's young life. He wanted to claim to be wiser for it; he wanted his hardships to give him leverage in life. But it wasn't worth it—he didn't want to be the next sob story.

Rather, he would gather up all his nevers: never went to prom with someone he loved, never brought home someone his parents approved of, never was included in the family business, never was accepted when he needed it. He took those nevers and wore them modestly. Like a sweater. When they became too hot for him, he would take them off and spend a day focused on some other farce like wrangling the children. Or chasing after Nanette. Or finding some peace before bed with Joey, a man who managed to subvert opposition.

But peace, that impossible circumstance, wouldn't find him soon. After all, he chose to work with kids.

Downstairs, Joey lay on the bed, staring up at the plaster beads on the ceiling, watching their shadows flicker and dance from the light of his scented candles.

There were no footsteps up above. Nanette probably fell asleep, not thinking anything of raising her voice with Rich. Whatever strange phase Nanette currently endured was likely contained. He hoped. If she wanted to be secretive then that was her prerogative. Probably, she would be less comfortable sleeping if she had revealed where she had been for that missing half-hour.

The shouting was too much for Joey. Because he couldn't get them to stop he couldn't stick around any longer than he had. Even then, he could see that after his untold exit that the argument had come to a close. It was like they were kids and would only throw a tantrum if they had an audience for it.

Maybe Rich was right. It might be time for them to move on from the fortress of Nanette Abbot. Nanette, apparently, was changing too. If she set herself on some new track then perhaps she wouldn't have all the space for him and Rich and their various business endeavors. She had, up until a few days ago, been a reliable creature of habit. And maybe Joey was waiting for this. A nudge. How long was he planning to live with his cousin anyway? If he wanted to start a family, he couldn't do that here.

He didn't like all this quiet anymore.

Rolling out of bed, Joey distractedly pulled on a pair of socks and traipsed up the stairs. The house was dark, but he had it memorized. Without lights he followed the railing up and across the landing. Making it to the kitchen door, he saw that the last person to exit hadn't shut it the whole way. Joey pushed it open enough to poke his head in.

The kitchen was shadowed like the rest of the house. A moonbeam through the window outlined one side of Rich, curled up on the kitchen floor. He wasn't crying; he didn't cry.

Joey's body was suspended. It was unusual for grand disputes to happen between any three of them. Let alone for them to have lasting consequences. Most of the time the solution was, "What can you do? It's Nanette." But today was weighted differently. He imagined going over and pulling Rich to him. He imagined whispering something kind, and something necessary, and something reassuring, but he didn't know what that would be and if a failed attempt would worsen the situation.

He leaned toward the kitchen, frozen in air.

But then he rocked back, taking steps away. He lowered his hand from the door. There was a percussion in his chest trying to beat its way out, as if they were younger again, little, like middle schoolers but in college when the start of something new in a relationship was so much louder than anything else.

This was the best he could do.

He left Rich to his own thoughts and walked back down the stairs. He pushed into their bedroom and wrapped the duvet around himself. He laid down on the mattress and began to count. Second by second, he wanted to know how many would pass before Rich would come down to bed.

Joey gave up though when he began repeating numbers.

The bedsheet burrito flopped onto its side and closed its eyes and waited for it to become a new day

CHAPTER SEVEN

JAVIER BOLIVAR

Fridays were pizza days. The guys ordered takeout for lunch every Friday to make up for the time they tried to make their own pizza and nearly had the microwave catch fire. Many of the children were giddy anticipating the end-of-week delight and hopped around the playroom, entertained by their mere excitement.

Among these happy hoppers was Javier Bolivar, who had forgotten again that it was pizza day. He forgot whenever it rolled around. He liked the forgetting aspect of exciting days because he got to experience the joy of learning the information twice. It was like being reminded that it was his birthday. Because Javier was still on the newer side, he didn't have many pizza days but the last one was fun—everybody was super energetic and then slept really well during the nap.

He had spent most of the morning being a patient for Doctors Figgy and Meadow who were exercising the new set of plastic doctor toys. He laid down on one of the yoga mats as the girls placed a blue stethoscope with a heart sticker on it to his forehead. "The good news is his heart is in the right place," said Doctor Figgy. Javier, by this time in his Baby Badger career, thought that he was finally fitting in with the others.

Sure, everyone seemed to know what was next on the schedule before him. And it felt as if not everybody remembered his name. But heck, he had made at least two strong friends and he was pretty sure that they liked each other.

Meadow took a plastic scalpel and stabbed it into Figgy's arm. Figgy then laughed, held up Meadow's imaginary medical license, and tore it in two.

From what Javier was able to tell about his best friends: everyone liked Figgy because she was always trying to be a friend, and no one really liked Meadow because she "knew" that everyone liked her the most and therefore didn't have to try. Javier could see through Meadow's arrogant exterior and tell that all she needed was a friend that she believed she already had had. So, as they waited for the notorious pizza man, the playroom was abuzz with anxious little doctors and explorers and leaders.

As Figgy used imaginary tape to mend Meadow's medical license, Javier sat up from his operating table. Off to the side he saw Yuki standing by herself. The Fieldings wouldn't have abandoned her; they were the nicest Badgers in the bunch. When Javier looked to her direction she would glance away, and when the reverse happened—in an effort to preserve the little girl's comfort—Javier would do the same. He thought to ask her what was wrong, but he didn't know if he could. Out of all the others at Baby Badger, he talked to Yuki and the Fieldings the least. Well, actually he talked to The Tenth the least but that hardly counted because everybody talked to The Tenth the least.

After Figgy sorted out the license dilemma, she saw Javier staring and asked him what was wrong.

"I think Yuki wants to play with us," he said.

"I got this," said Meadow. Then turning to Yuki she said, "Leave us alone, baby."

Figgy groaned Meadow's name while approaching Yuki. She, being much taller than the toddler, got on her knees to talk. "Hi, Yuki, do you want to play with us?"

"Sorry," the littlest said. She sucked in a breath of air and scurried out of the playroom. The seven-year-olds traded perplexed expressions in the following seconds.

"Weird," Meadow said.

"Is she okay?" Javier asked.

"Why don't you ask Roux?"

"Meadow," Figgy snapped.

"I'm sorry."

"Should we get back to the operation?"

"I dunno. I'm kinda tired with the hospital."

"Javy, what do you want to do?"

"I'm okay for anything."

Figgy and Meadow then argued for what the last activity would be before lunch time. Javier got comfortable as the argument commenced because he had heard enough of them to tell that it may be long enough to bring them all the way to lunch time. He looked over at the twins who were messing about with a large collection of toy trucks, and then over at The Tenth who appeared to be chewing on the ear of a Pokèmon plush. After a couple minutes, Jon came in and cleaned up some of the things that nobody was playing with before vanishing again.

Whenever the girls fought, it usually spawned from Javier not making a decision. He was fine with voicing his preference if Figgy or Meadow each had something particular they wanted to accomplish, but more often Javier didn't go into the day with a specific agenda or game he wanted to carry out. Once, Meadow accosted him for never wanting to do anything and he just shut down and cried. Javier wished that he had something that he wanted to do, but those things ended up being less tangible than a game—he wanted everybody to have a turn doing what they wanted. Sometimes, he thought Figgy and Meadow wanted to argue simply because they liked arguing. But then that would be silly. Who argues for the sake of arguing?

A car pulled up in front of the building.

Because the windows were higher up on the walls in the playroom, the Badgers needed other ways to look out and satisfy their curiosity. Zola and Virginia pushed in a footrest from the other room while Javier tried to help hoist Meadow enough to see out to the street.

The kids saw the promised spoils of a delivery girl walking up to the house with her famous pizza box-shaped bag. Before Mister Rich could even announce that it was lunch time, the kids were hurrying up the stairs.

Rich and Joey thought the pizza day setup was a blessing. The kids excite themselves silly all day, so that immediately after lunch they're too exhausted to do anything but sleep.

The guys were grinding up the nuggets, brushing the powdery, pale viridian meshes into Ziploc bags. They were listening to the low volume sounds of Rich's musical theatre playlist and the monitor where the relaxed breathing and whispers of the kids' voices came through from the other room. Rich squeezed shut one of the bags, undid it, and then tried it again. He was watching the corner where the ceiling met the wall, looking past it as if it were the open sky. Rich sat on the floor beside the bed. The apathy of the activity had been so palpable it brought Joey to remember back to college when he and Rich were eager to do this—to make enough money so they could go out and watch some new Wes Anderson movie, or that time they rented a tandem bike because they liked the idea of how stupid it would look. But the only Wes Anderson they saw recently was *Fantastic Mister Fox* and they could hardly get out long enough to do some niche outdoor activity. Frankly, the daycare did so well they didn't even need to sell the parents drugs anymore.

Joey didn't know if he felt guilty. After all, it was Massachusetts: weed was barely illegal and more likely taboo.

And now, as Rich bagged, Joey wondered where it had all gone. The magic. Whatever happened to the magic of it all? When was the last time they went to Denny's at two in the morning while high? When was the last time they fell asleep in the middle of making out only to wake up giggling? When did

Denny's become a monthly brunch and making out a before-bed kiss? Why were they so much older than their age? Were they stagnating?

At the same time, Rich found himself somewhat preoccupied with the thought of his little sister's upcoming birthday party. Despite his better inclinations, he wanted to go—to be a part of that old, first family of his. But he wasn't brave enough to go alone, and his brother made it clear that he shouldn't bring Joey. If he was brave enough, he'd show up with Joey anyway and force them to see him for who he was.

Joey thought about how funny Grandmother would find all of this. *Oh, you boys, so much life ahead of you. You shouldn't fret so much.* And yet here they were.

By the turn of the twentieth minute, Joey, who had been absently sitting at the desk, spoke up. "I've decided that this is bullshit."

"I made that desk, don't call it bullshit."

"No, not the desk, Rich—why would you think I meant the desk—" Rich stammered, "I'm trying to have an epiphany here."

"Go ahead."

"When's the last time we smoked?"

"We are not smoking right now."

"I know that. That wasn't the question."

"Oh okay. Um, Valentine's Day?"

"No because Nanette's parents took us out, remember?"

"Don't tell me it was New Year's. That was so long ago."

"I won't tell you it was New Year's, because it wasn't."

Rich wracked his mind for the answer. "Christmas?"

"Christmas."

"But that was at least six months ago!"

"At least."

"What's your point? Are we due?"

"My point is . . . I dunno," Joey said. Maybe we don't need to do this anymore."

"Give up ... gardening?"

"Maybe get a real one. You know, with perennials and

shit. Like we talked about?"

Joey's voice, usually even, was unsteady. His normal penchant was for making the days go by unchangingly. But as he sat back, staring at his glowing closet with the plastic tents and troughs of soil, he couldn't deny the utter apathy he felt for that branch of his enterprise. Rich sat up. He agreed with the moving-on that he hoped would be coming, but it was so unlike Joey to want something like this. Rich wondered what was happening to the Abbots. He thought it was only Nanette, but maybe there was something in the blood that unseated both of them. It was just far more likely that Joey would have a quieter derailment than that of his cousin.

But, in the end, this was a worrisome boon. Hopefully, Joey's hypothetical real garden would involve a house of their own, a family of their own. Maybe they could hire a snappy teenager to help them watch after the kids and they'd be legitimate businessmen.

After a moment, Rich asked, "So do we stop selling?"

"We should give them some notice. A week. Two weeks. In two weeks we stop selling. Forever."

Rich had just finished bagging. His frenetic fingers now tapped against his side. Two weeks! *C'est magnifique!* He smiled at Joey and then playfully commanded, "Come kiss me."

"Are you sure?" Joey chuckled. "You don't want me to finish up here first?"

"I'm positive."

Joey rose from the desk and floated over to his partner. As he got closer, the abrupt bells of a cellphone alarm erupted in the bedroom, overpowering the subtle tones of the music. Of course, they thought: Naptime was over.

When Nanette got home, Rich sat her down beside him at the kitchen table. He had been flipping through the intricate sketches of airplanes drawn into a notebook that Zola Dodd forgot when her parents came to pick her up. He found each new sketch astounding and far beyond the capability of a regular five-year-old. She would have to take it back on Monday. Nanette sat perfectly upright with both of her hands flat against her sides. They would've been on the tabletop, like how she sits in her office, but it was sticky and she didn't know from what. She assured Rich that whatever it was he needed to talk about it could wait. She watched as the parents to the girls with three feet between them and the nanny of the loud girl delivered the kleptomaniac children from her home.

Nanette hadn't seen it before, but now she was hoping that the snacks Joey fixed for the parents would take more time to prepare, whenever he handed them a snack they always pocketed it quickly with little regard the squashing or smooshing. She tried to make it to her car fast enough to follow one of these families home, but they moved so quickly. If just one thing took a bit more time, the fixing of a snack per se, then she could do it all without an issue. The kitchen stank of lingering cheesy grease and the trash was filled with stained paper plates that were crushed and warped in shape. She couldn't discern whether or not the bulb in the chandelier was flickering or rather her eye just had a twitch.

"Netty," Rich said, his elbows on the table as he leaned toward her, "I want to apologize for yesterday."

"Yes, well, we all could have seen this one coming, Richard. All the same, I accept your apology but will not reciprocate it because frankly I have done nothing wrong. What do you say we let these bygones be proverbial bygones?"

"I was hoping we could try for more of a conversation, Nanette. We don't just have to tolerate each other because of Joey. We can try to get along."

The doorbell rang. Nanette listened to Joey receive the visitors. *Hey, Con, Javy was a delight today. Would you like to come in for a second? I have a snack for you.* And then, *That sounds great, Joe, I think I will.*

"Yes, I suppose we can try… however the word unto itself stinks of the possibility of failure."

"I'm trying to be nice here, Nanette," Rich said patiently. "We won't be here forever, so might as well make the most of our time."

Nanette's head snapped to meet Rich's gaze.

"What do you mean you would not be here forever?"

"I mean we won't be here forever."

"Are you ill?"

"No, just… you knew we wouldn't stay here forever."

"Yes… I of course knew that. In fact, I am surprised you have mooched off my hospitality for this long. How many years have we sustained each other's company? Ten? Ten years?"

"Two, Nanette."

"Yes, well, I suppose it just feels like ten years. If time flies when one has fun, then I suppose the opposite must be true as well."

Joey entered the kitchen, fiddled about the cabinets for a specific Tupperware container, and left. Nanette's head bounced back and forth between the two boys. She wondered if leaving was Joey's decision. Then she heard: *Alright, Con, see you Monday. Have a fun weekend, Javy!* Nanette shot up from her seat and headed for the door to the garage.

"Phenomenal speech as per usual, Rich. We really should do this more often, truly. Unfortunately… I left the iron on at the, the, office. And we just cannot have that whole, uh, building burn down now, can we? I am sure you understand."

"Come on, Nanette, an iron? Why can't you just talk?"

"Unavoidable!"

She disappeared behind the door.

Rich sat alone at the kitchen table. He got up to stare at the door to the garage. He reached for the knob, but his hand fell away. On his way back to his seat, he felt an impulse rush through him and followed through the door.

The Bolivar home always smelled of cumin. Abuela used it in every single one of her recipes. Always. Peanut butter and jelly? Bam. Cumin. She had these shamanistic tendencies to invent cures and spells to fight against the inevitable superstitions of the age. She was the matriarch of the Bolivar clan and so when she said ingesting cumin was the only way to ensure a lucky day then you bucked up and ate some cumin.

Her son, Leon, and his wife, Con, had found ways around the curative insistence of cumin—Abuela didn't seem to see when they occasionally replaced her powdered cumin shaker with one filled with a flavorless substitute of the same color. However, as defeated as the younger Bolivars were, they probably couldn't even taste it anymore.

Friends of the Bolivar children developed a running joke about the home: It doesn't matter where you are, Abuela's cumin to get you.

Con pulled into the little parking lot of the condominium. They lived in a building with two other units and never saw their neighbors. Beside the stone steps leading up to the door were a couple of metal trash cans underneath the window. She took her son by the hand, all the while asking him things about his day, but when she got inside her demeanor shifted. The change was invisible to Javier. She began saying, "You're going to spend time with your sisters. They are going to watch you upstairs where you can play some video games with them until eight. Because at eight it's bedtime and you're going to sleep and have some sweet dreams In the morning you're getting up early because it's the last day of Sunday School and next year you can finally go to Sunday School on Sundays because Papi has the time to drive you. Mercedes! Crissie! Come play with your brother! And, Javy, you know I'm right downstairs if you need me."

She kissed him on the forehead as his sisters hurried down the stairs to pick him up. Con left for the kitchen where she figured she'd find Leon and his mother. The three Bolivar children went up the stairs to be left to their video games.

Nanette's head appeared in the window. Her eyes darted around, taking inventory of the inside of the condo.

As was her standard, she hoped for the negligence of the

family to leave the front door unlocked. Nanette had developed a protocol in the reconnaissance missions now and every step required the door to be fortuitously unlocked. Noting that the foyer was devoid of human life, Nanette approached the front door and tried the handle. She heard a soft click and, just like that, she was inside. *The carelessness of these families*, Nanette thought, *it's a good thing that it's me entering their homes instead of some neurotic burglar.*

The first thing to happen inside the Bolivar residence was that Nanette nearly passed out from the overwhelming stench of spice. The gust invaded her nostrils and tried to burst out of her head from the inside. She faltered over to the wall, using it to prop herself up. Nanette hit the wall with a *thud*. Fearing it was loud enough to compromise the operation, she froze. Listening in, she heard: *I am, I am, Leon, it was probably just the kids—I'll check. Start mixing the batter—and you better not have confused the stuff with cumin like last time because your mother was the only one who liked that.*

A door creaked open at the end of the hall. Capture was imminent. Nanette bolted up the stairs, hopping on the pads of her feet. She ducked around the corner out of sight from the bottom of the stairs.

"Kids, you better be playing nice!" she yelled up.

From what Nanette could tell, the kids didn't hear their mother. Some new-age, boppy, electric music pulsed through the door right across from her where, she presumed, the children were summoning their god Skrillex or whatever it was that they did. Javier's sisters were actually playing *Super Mario Galaxy 2* but none of those words would have made any sense to Nanette either.

She pulled herself up off the ground.

The musical door cracked open and out stepped Javier. He was the only one of the Bolivar kids that thought they heard their mother shout something.

"Miss Nan—?" Before Javier could finish saying her name, she moved him away from the doorway and pulled the door shut behind him. She glared at him placing one extended finger over her mouth and shushing him. But he still asked, "Miss Nanette?"

"Quiet, child. You should not have seen me."

"What are you doing here?"

"Like you don't know."

"Should I know?"

"Where is the lunchbox?"

"My lunchbox is in the kitchen."

"Not yours. Mine."

"It might be in the kitchen."

"Tell me something I do not know."

"The echidna is the only mammal that lays eggs."

"What?" Nanette froze for a second, amazed at the possibility that there was a mammal capable of laying eggs. Then she narrowed her eyes. He was trying to distract her. "What do you want?"

"What do you mean?"

"What are you going to do? Sell me out?"

"I dunno."

"You are not telling me that you are just going to let me walk."

He shrugged. "Wait long enough, people choose things for you."

"So you're going to do nothing?"

"I was going to go play *Super Mario*."

"Then you did not see me here today."

"Okay."

Javier receded back into the musical room. Nanette, seeing how she did not believe in luck, congratulated herself for conquering another perilous situation thanks to her unparalleled wits. Treading airily, she tiptoed back down the stairs. She discerned that the kitchen was at the end of this foyer, but it was filled with parents.

Before she formulated a solid plan, there was a tap on the window.

Looking through it at her she saw Rich's head, horrified. Nanette didn't know what he had to be so horrified about but she figured that it wasn't good that she'd been found out. Wrath on his face, Rich mouthed, *What are you doing here?*

Nanette mouthed in return, *You are going to ruin everything.*

Get out of there. Are you freaking insane?

Leave me be. I know what I'm doing.

How could you possibly know what you're doing?!

Oh, so know we are just going to go ahead and question my tact, are we? Hello, wounds! You need a little more salt in you.

Get. Out. Here. Now.

I. Am. Not. Finished. Yet.

WITH WHAT?

Don't shout! Jiminy cricket, do we want the whole building on our heels?

In fury, Rich backed away from the window to pace a circle. His miscalculated his distance from the metal trashcans and toppled right over them. The percussive clattering that followed compelled Nanette to dive into the nearby coat closet. At the same time, sensing peril, Rich booked it up the street. The Bolivar parents sprinted through the foyer and out onto the front steps. Nanette heard them blame neighborhood teens while she broke out of the closet and squirmed into the kitchen.

In the corner, there was an elderly Spanish woman asleep with a shaker of cumin in her hand. The countertop beside the oven had brownie mix all over it. Next to a large container labeled CUMIN, Nanette saw a plastic bag filled with oddly colored cumin. On the farthest wall there was a door that led to the backstreet.

Not wasting any more time, she scoured the few cabinets. The kitchen was tiny for six people. Inside of the refrigerator housed no lunchbox, nor did the top. The cabinets beside the range were filled with packages of tortillas and some cans of SpaghettiOs and, much to Nanette's dismay, had several lunchboxes for the children of the home though none of which resembled the lunchbox. Nanette perceived she only had moments left and there was only one cabinet left to open. . . but it was blocked by the knee of sleeping Abuela.

Gingerly (well, as gingerly as Nanette was capable) she pushed the leg aside. The loose skin of the calf nearly billowed in the breeze. With her other hand, Nanette cracked open the final cabinet and saw every other spice crammed in with loose plastic containers for food.

Nanette slammed the door shut just a little too hard. The noise jostled the woman awake: Nanette watched in slow motion as Abuela's eyes blinked open.

"Who are you?" Abuela sneered.

After half of a second, Nanette managed, "I'm with the grocery store… Did your order of cumin arrive in three business days or, uh, less?"

"Yes it did," she grinned, proud.

"Thank you for your input, I'll see myself out."

She scooted out onto the backstreet and ducked out of view from any window.

Nanette celebrated and mourned—another complete battle in the war of investigation. As she snuck back to her car, she found Rich leaning against the driver's side door.

His arms were crossed, his foot was tapping.

Chapter Eight

ZOLA AND VIRGINIA DODD

A breeze blew between Nanette and Rich, overturning the leaves on the trees. Neither one of them knew quite what the other was up to.

"Thank goodness it is Friday, am I r-right?" Nanette tried.

"What in the everlasting hell was that, Nanette?" Rich asked.

"You see, that there was this societal convention known as small talk and I thought I might have myself a go at it."

"So you just break into homes now? Is this how you pass your time? The Bolivars are our friends and they pay us so we can live. Plus they have children. Imagine how scarring it would be for kids to see you snooping around their home?"

"Yes, I imagine it would be scarring if a child happened to see me."

"Did anyone see you?"

"I am not a fan of this inquisition, Richard. Your questions insinuate that I am not proficient in this."

"Proficient—have, have, have you done this before?" His hands flailed as he repeated his words in the effort to settle on his question.

Nanette became preoccupied with a rock at her feet.

"Oh my god, you have. You've broken into other houses. Which? Which houses have you broken into?"

"I hardly see how this is your business—"

"Cut the crap, Nanette, this is serious. Which houses?"

"Only one."

"This one, right?"

"What? No. This was a condominium."

"Jesus Christ. How many houses have you broken into?"

"None."

"Nanette, I know you love semantics and your idea of breaking-in may be different from mine but tell me. How many places have you been in?"

"Three."

"Oh god."

"So far, at least."

"Oh god."

"A house, an apartment, and a condominium. I did not break into anywhere because so far the families have thankfully been negligent enough to leave the front doors unlocked."

"I'm living with a lunatic."

Nanette paused to wonder why Rich would have brought up Joey at this point.

"You won't be telling Joseph about this, correct?" she asked.

"Why," Rich pressed his face to his palm, "why wouldn't I tell him about this?"

"I do not see why he would need to know. Frankly, you knowing is rather hazardous."

"Who were the other homes? Were they people we know?"

"No."

"You sure?"

"*We* didn't know them. You and Joseph know them much better than I do. There was an argumentative sort of couple and then some artsy types that seemed disenchanted by their craft."

"Christ. The Greens and the Allaways."

"Never caught their names."

"This has to stop. Like this has to stop right now."

"Ha. What's next, Rich? Would you like me to reason with an avalanche to get it to walk back up the hill?"

"What's this about? Why do you need this?"

"I do not need to break into children's homes. I am not some deranged adrenaline junkie, mind you."

"Then why?"

"What is the likelihood of this conversation ending without you receiving your answer?"

"About the same as me ratting you out to Joey in a minute."

"You would not dare."

"Try me, Netty."

They listened to the leaves rustle in the gale.

"If you must know, Richard, I'm uncovering the whereabouts of my lunchbox."

"Your lunch—?!" It appeared like Rich had just been punched in the stomach as he doubled over beside Nanette's car. Three minutes passed with him collecting himself. "You can just buy a new lunchbox."

"Nonsense. And spend eternity wondering what vagrant wandered off with my property? The notion of it all is laughable."

"You're talking about kids here, Nanette. If one of them has your lunchbox then why wouldn't we just ask the parents to check for us?"

"You expect me to believe that these parents wouldn't lie through their teeth to protect their, their, their progeny? They're hardly an impartial party here, Richard."

"It's not like you'd press charges!"

"Why would I not? Stolen property, Rich, stolen property."

"They're children!"

"Everybody has to learn sometime!"

"I'm telling Joey."

Rich stepped away from Nanette's car door, but she

blocked his path. He couldn't sidestep her.

"You should not do that, Rich."

"Why shouldn't I?"

"I will half your rent next month."

"Won't that just look suspicious? You can't bribe me, Nanette."

"I am not doing anything uncouth or unjust here, Richard. Just. Just. Is there anything you want? A new rug? Tickets to see *Wicked* for the twentieth time?"

"I don't like your tone—*Wicked* is one of the most successful musicals in the world right now and is more successful than you or I could ever be. Also, shut up."

"Is there really nothing?"

Rich held his position. Nanette never fought for anything like help. She built the world she wanted to exist in and then forced other people to tolerate it. The fact that she needed him was too delicious for him to pass on.

"I may have something," Rich admitted, "but you might not like it."

"What made you assume I would have enjoyed anything about our present situation?"

"My family's throwing a birthday party."

"No."

"For my little sister."

"No."

"And I need a … female companion."

"Good luck."

"Nanette. You're not in a position to make requests."

"You are sure about that? Why would you even want to spend time with those paper-made aristocrats? I have enough ill will toward my own family to start disavowing yours. I would imagine you would go by yourself before taking me with you."

"Nanette, you know well enough that if that was a possibility I would take it a million times before I would want to be seen with you by my family."

"That's the sweetest thing you've said to me."

"But they need to see me in a certain light."

"You want to lie to them. I hate liars."

"You've been lying all week."

"Yes, but I know how to do it."

"You're a hypocrite!"

"How am I to know that you can even keep up such a ruse? Has that even occurred to you? What if you get there and cannot even fathom the perpetuation of this lie? Of reforming your non-reformable ways to this family that turned their back to you?"

"Because I can!"

"No dice, Richard. Deceiving the stationary magnate of New England is a job for some other unsuspecting woman."

"Then I dunno, Nanette. I'm not going to take the time to prove myself to you."

He began to walk again, and again Nanette stopped his path.

"Maybe you could prove yourself," she said.

"What?"

"Prove that you can pull off a heist like the one you need from me."

Nanette smiled uncomfortably—as if she wasn't really acquainted with how a human person typically smiled. Rich narrowed his eyes. He began to have a complete understanding of Nanette's seedy intentions.

"You aren't..." Rich trailed. "I won't..."

"You will, Richard."

"I can't."

"You can and you shall. Join me, Richard. At least for a day."

"You're insane."

"Talk is tough, Richard. But I am tougher."

"You... insane."

Though, as the words flittered away in the comforting summer breeze, Rich examined the devious intent upon Nanette's face and couldn't help but wonder: What did happen to that lunchbox?

Joey slept amazingly. He chalked it up to having the house to himself for a few minutes the night before. As he woke up, he found Rich easily shaken. Joey calmed Rich, urging him to go back to sleep as he got on with his day.

Sleeping in used to be essential for all of Joey's days off. But, since his heavily stoned college days, Joey realized he slept through too many appointments and sustained too many verbal lectures from professors, employers, academic advisors, and his own parents, to feel comfortable sleeping away the entire morning. He spent his first hour cooking enough pancakes to have breakfast for him and Rich for the whole week. Saturdays were also Nanette's shopping day. She liked to take care of all the groceries because she was the only person trustworthy enough to not forget something like Rich's Greek yogurt or her need for there to be at least thirty clementines in the house at any given moment.

If she was up already, he couldn't tell. Nanette's weekend morning of lumbering about was no different from her weekday mornings. Relaxation was a moot concept to her, as she was most relaxed when she had twenty things to do at any given instance.

He took inventory of the countertops as he tidied up. Most interesting an inclusion to the day's clutter was Zola Dodd's notebook which held many a mind-blowing illustration. The Dodds were the second and third most likely children to keep to themselves at Baby Badger, after the Tenth Child, of course. It seemed as a result of keeping themselves busy, they produced some of the most unique innovations that playtime was able to spawn. If the Fieldings created a kingdom, then the Dodds could automate it.

Rich walked into the kitchen then, his hair riddled with the flyaway locks of a restless night. Pausing for a brief moment—it was like the sight of the notebook had triggered a far-off memory—he bid Joey good morning with a kiss on his cheek.

"You should go back to bed," Joey advised.

"I wouldn't be able to sleep anyway."

"Why are you so far gone this morning?"

"No reason. Hey. Do you think Zola will miss her notebook?"

"Yeah, probably. But it can wait 'til Monday."

There was a light series of knocks on the front door that vaguely resembled the beat to the finale of Tchaikovsky's 1812 Overture. Answering it, Joey found the tiny personage of Grandmother Abbot. She smiled, went through her usual hellos, and came inside. However, though it was her custom to come up to the kitchen or living room and have tea brought to her, Grandmother took her introductory instances to descend the stairs.

"Whoa, Gran, where're you heading?" Joey asked, stumbling down the stairs trying to get in front of her.

"Well, Joey, it is such a lovely morning that I thought I'd get an early start."

She turned into the playroom and opened up the miniscule trunks of the play cars. Then she moved onto the box filled with the yoga mats next to one of the toy boxes. She tore through the collections of childish fancies with precision, making sure that she put everything back tidier than its original state.

"Early start for what?" Joey coughed. "If I can ask."

"I'm looking for Netty's lunchbox, Joey."

By this time, Rich was standing a couple yards away, trying to listen as intently as he could. Appearing behind him was Nanette who, though it was but eight o'clock on a Saturday morning, was already dressed in her daily suit.

"Is it a smidgen cold in here, Rich?" Nanette asked.

"No?"

"Funny. And here I was: thinking hell hath frozen over. What is this woman doing in my house on a Saturday?"

She didn't wait for an answer. Rather as Nanette closed in on the way to the playroom, Grandmother zoomed by her with Joey following thereafter. Grandmother floated to Joey and Rich's bedroom and, before anyone else could intercept, entered. The door to the closet was shut, but the bed was unmade, and the guys' clothes from the day before were just scattered across the ground.

Nanette, Joey, and Rich clotted the threshold all in attempts to remove Grandmother from the vicinity. They struggled to release themselves from the others in the doorway while Grandmother went around picking up and folding the dirty clothes on the floor.

Joey slipped away from the pack and placed himself between Grandmother and the closet door. And Nanette, upon regaining the freedom of movement, went to grab her Grandmother by the shoulders—but when she lifted her hands, Grandmother leered at Nanette causing them to flail about in open air before landing haphazardly at her sides.

"Morning, Nanette," Grandmother chirped.

"So it is. I had not noticed. Listen, Grandmother, would you not be more inclined to will away your final Saturdays in some Bingo hall or baking class rather than reorganizing my perfectly orderly home?"

"I'm here for you, Netty. I'm looking for your lunchbox."

"Oh, bless! The cavalry's arrived. Let me ask you this, Grandmother. Under which ill consideration did you contrive that I would not have already searched my own home?"

Grandmother, in her regular breezy ways that terrified Nanette so, placed her stack of folded laundry down on the corner of the bed. Turning to Joey, she asked, "Boys, would be so kind as to give us some time alone?"

The query blindsided Joey, he stammered before managing, "Wouldn't you two be more comfortable upstairs?" He saw Rich mouthing his name from across the room.

"We'll only be a minute, dear."

"Yes well," said Nanette, "if it's the only way."

"Are you two sure?" Joey tried. "It's so much more comfortable upstairs."

"Do not worry, Joseph," Nanette said. "It's not like you have anything to hide."

On the word hide Nanette did something rather strange: she winked. This, of course, was to signify that there was something to hide and she, for the first time, was in on the secret. One could tell it was her first time being in on a secret because as she winked she followed up with a clumsy rotation of her shoulder. It was not subtle. This bewildered Joey as he tried to figure out what she could know about the secret of the garden. Then he remembered that Nanette knew there was a statue of a naked Joey Abbot in there rather than a dubious collection of cannabis plants.

With his better judgement screaming at him from the other side of the house, Joey said, "Okay. Just a couple minutes."

"Joey…" Rich whispered as Joey joined him in the doorway. Rich looked over his shoulder as Joey pulled him into the hall. And with a click, Nanette and Grandmother were by themselves.

Nanette wouldn't meet her Grandmother's eyes. She fixated on the stray beads of thread that poked up out of the carpet, hoping that the seconds she counted were viable towards the minute in hell to which she submitted.

"I am not against you, Nanette. I am on your side. Always and forever."

"Redundant. Always and forever."

"Don't be like that."

"I will be however I want to be in my home."

"Just let me help you."

"Help me do what? Dismantle all I have worked for? You come in and search my house as if I was an incompetent dolt unable to discern the whereabouts of my own lunchbox. If it was on my property than I assure you that it would have been located by now."

"You've even searched Joseph's room?"

"Yes."

"Every inch."

"More or less, but I am sure you get the gist of my thorough faculties."

Grandmother moved a pillow out of the way as she sat on the bed. She was impressed with her little girl, moving beyond her former self and finding solutions that she would have previously missed. Nanette countered her by walking across the room, stopping in front of the desk.

"Nanette," Grandmother said. "Nanette look at me."

She did.

"I'm proud of you. In the past, things like this would break you. I see you've grown."

"Yes, yes. Thank you, pride, all that, we really should be going."

"Will you let me be proud of you? Ever since—"

"Ever since nothing! We need not go into the errors of our pasts now. Right, Grandmother?"

"Stop interrupting me. Just because you're afraid of the events of your—"

"The hand puppet fiasco was ten years ago. It has passed."

"You know I don't mean the hand puppet fiasco."

Grandmother stood up as she spoke. She inventoried the boys' room as if calculating all the potential possibilities of their lives that had been wasted, squandered, or that had yet to come. As if wondering if they would rise above this basement room or if another tempest would keep them swamped to the ground. Or maybe she just had gas.

She looked back to Nanette, and then beyond her.

"Have you checked that closest?"

"Wha-what? What closet? This closet? Yes I have. Oh, the time I have spent checking this closet in particular."

"Closets can be tricky. What if we looked through it together? For old time's sake."

"Joseph and Richard, I could not imagine, would be too fond of that."

"Please? For your old grandmother?"

Grandmother made a step toward the closet door and Nanette stepped with her. Behind her back, Nanette's hands fumbled for the handle to the door. She wanted to secure it.

"You said it yourself," Grandmother said, "what do the boys have to hide?"

Grandmother took another step toward Nanette and Nanette pressed herself up against the closed door as if she was held there magnetically. She clenched her teeth, uncomfortable with the notion of seeing the nude rendition of her cousin.

"Here's what we can do!" Nanette yelped. "I will go in"—this pained her somewhat to say—"and report back in a jiffy."

"Well, okay."

Grandmother took a step back. Nanette realized she had been holding her breath. But, as she prepared herself to see a most unwelcoming rendition of Joseph Abbot, opened the door and whipped it shut behind her. She wondered why the room was so dark, only to recognize that she had latched her eyes shut. Without questioning the buzzing of the lights, or the dirt scent of the room, Nanette counted to thirty with her eyes held closed before stepping out and gasping.

"It's not in there," she reported.

"A shame." Grandmother shook her head. "I'll keep an eye out."

"I am sure you will. Make sure you tell us when you are leaving town."

"And Nanette. . . you really should talk to Joseph."

"I will never tell him. And neither will you."

"Will I not?"

"I will never tell him, but I would bludgeon myself senseless before you got the chance."

An iota of cordiality between them, they exited the bedroom.

To keep from fidgeting, Joey left to mow the grass. After Nanette saw Grandmother out the front door, she went into her en suite and took a shower fully clothed. Afterwards she changed into her backup Saturday suit and tried to go about her weekend as she would normally. Nanette forced herself to recognize that, with no kids at the daycare on the weekend, she had no idea where any of the children lived. And therefore she was unable to make progress in her spreadsheet which now had three entries to it.

Rich, all the while, sat in the kitchen listening to classical music and tapping his fingers against the cover to Zola's notebook. Tomorrow was his sister's birthday party and, though he didn't have a date, he hadn't given up hope. Nanette came into the kitchen and poured herself a glass of milk. She drank it while staring out the window above the sink and tried to remember simpler times.

Rich didn't look at her when he spoke. "Your grandmother leave?"

"Yes. Luckily the three other horsemen waited for her."

An instance, reticent.

"Can't find your lunchbox on a weekend," Rich toyed with her. Tap, tap, tapping the notebook cover.

"I will make do."

"Can't make do if you don't know their addresses."

"You can be helpful, Richard, and supply them to me."

"No. That's too much power."

"What would you suggest?"

"You need me. If I help you, I expect you to return the favor."

"I do not need anyone, let alone a disgraceful mooch."

"Forty-eight hours at least until some child gets picked up. You think you can wait that long? Sitting passively in the unknown?"

Nanette put her glass down. Wiping her milk mustache from her upper lip, she faltered. "What would you suggest?"

"We do this my way."

"No deal."

"I'm not negotiating."

She loathed him in that moment—no, wait, it might actually have been respect.

Joey came in from mowing the yard sopping with sweat. It was a beautiful day, especially for watching Netflix with Rich. He saw Nanette's car veering round the turtle in the street and driving down the lane to go grocery shopping, as was her Saturday custom. He stripped off his T-shirt and listened for movement in the house. "Rich?" he called. "Rich?"

Zola and Virginia shared a bedroom. It was a nice bedroom on the second floor of the home. Up against the back wall were the bunkbeds where Zola had claimed the top and Virginia the bottom. Months before, their dad invested in that fancy whiteboard paint and transformed an entire wall of the bedroom into an Expo canvas. The whiteboard wall became their central for brainstorms Along the walls were collections of Lego bricks, folded up easels, 3D puzzles, and a couple collections of book series next to an unfinished IKEA bookshelf. There were boxes with brushes and little tubes of paint, pouches with colored pencils and erasers of every shape, stacks of finished coloring books, and even larger stacks of well-loved sketchbooks. The Dodds, if anything, were thorough. They exhausted one activity in its entirety before finding something new, and their books were no different. Every page of a sketchbook or notebook was completely employed before they could justify a new one.

There wasn't a laptop or television in the girls' bedroom. There was only one in the house but it didn't have cable. It was there so the kids could play *Minecraft* if they wanted to, or if their parents wanted to watch a movie with the whole family, including the Dodd twins' two much older brothers (each with his own bedroom).

Presently, the girls were drawing on the whiteboard sketches of what appeared to be grappling hooks. At Baby Badger, a lot of the kids were into playing spies or robbers and though the pretending didn't quite appeal to the girls, the mechanics of the make-believe did. From what they drew so far, the hardest part for them to envision was the actual hook.

They couldn't discern whether they should go with one crook or three. But what was worse was that they failed to decide on what the hook would be made out of. Zola sat on her bed surrounded by Legos. She was putting the pieces together in a prototype hook. She tied it to one of their mother's scarves and tested it by attempting to catch it on the safety bar of Virginia's bunk. It caught just fine, but when she applied any weight to it the hook just fell apart.

On the other end of the room, Virginia was sketching out various shapes for the hook to take. She was the more methodical of the girls. Whereas Zola wanted to get to the practical testing first, Virginia wanted to present all their options up front. They traded off from day to day whose approach was better for whichever project.

Zola saw that Virginia was stretching as far as she could to write on the part of the whiteboard they were too short to fully reach on their own. She grabbed the footstool out of the clutter along the wall and brought it over to her sister.

"Here," Zola said.

"I got it," Virginia replied.

"I'm just helping."

"I got it."

Virginia wobbled atop the footstool, constantly shooing away her spotting sister. Zola didn't trust Virginia's prosthetic foot because they didn't make it themselves. Even when they presented alternatives to their parents, they weren't allowed to switch up what the foot was. In solidarity, Zola offered to give Virginia one of her feet—but their parents kiboshed that idea just as quickly. It had been six months since Virginia lost her foot and the only ones still adjusting were their parents.

Roland, one of the brothers, walked through the open door and told his little sisters that lunch was ready and that Mama wasn't going to wait like last night. The twins dropped their current preoccupations. Virginia stepped off the stool, passively rejecting her sister's offer to help. The rejection wasn't mean—Virginia liked that her sister was there for her, but she couldn't articulate that she needed to be self-sufficient.

Moments later, Zola, Virginia, and Roland sat at the island in the kitchen to eat Mama's eggplant parm. It was a new recipe because almost all of Mama's recipes were new recipes. The eldest brother, Everett, was not there because his father took him to tryouts for his soccer summer camp. Mama doled out the food liberally even though it seemed that only the parents gained weight in this household.

A couple minutes into lunch, knocking at the door off the side of the kitchen was Mister Rich Eliot. He was smiling and waving through the window. Misses Dodd sprung to receive him, wiping her hands on her apron. She welcomed him into the house with an offer of eggplant parm and a seat.

"I'm good, thank you," Mister Rich said, as if regarding an old friend.

"To what do we owe the pleasure?" Misses Dodd asked.

"Mister Rich!" Zola shouted. She hopped down from her seat and went to assist her sister. With a roll of her eyes, Virginia took Zola's hand and hopped to the floor.

"Hey, girls," he beamed.

"Is Mister Joey with you?" Virginia asked.

"No, it's just me today." The girls had been circling him and when they heard this news they slowed down, but didn't stop. "I'm here because a certain somebody forgot something."

He held up Zola's notebook. At the sight of it, the girls chirped with giggles and gratitude like chicks being fed by a mother bird.

"You came all this way," Misses Dodd said pleasantly, "just to bring my girl back her little doodles. And on the weekend too! You are too kind, Richard. Will you at least let me give you a little tour?"

"Oh, I don't know if I have the time…"

"It's not too big a house, now. Kids help me tidy up the hall."

"Really, Emmalee, it's…"

Rich trailed off because he was the only one in the room to see Nanette Abbot's head appear in the window to the front yard. He shot daggers at her fast enough to make her duck out of the view.

Misses Dodd turned and asked, "What are you looking at?"

"Hey, I will have that tour."

"Lovely! Let's tidy up real quick."

Emmalee Dodd led her kids out of the kitchen and left Rich by himself. He ran over to the front window and opened it.

"The plan was for you to stay in the car," he lectured.

Nanette replied from behind a hedge, "And leave you to mess it up? Never."

"So you prefer to mess things up by yourself, is it?"

"I do not mess it up! I carry on fine by myself."

"Go back to the car!"

"Look for my lunchbox!"

Rich slammed the window shut. Scurrying over to the pantry, he held his hand over the handle. He was faster to pull his hand away than he was to grab ahold. After a couple frozen seconds of tentative not-really-much-happening, Rich touched the pantry door only for Mrs, Dodd to reenter the kitchen.

"Such craftsmanship," Rich said, stroking the woodwork. He turned to her, "Is this an heirloom of sorts?"

"It's from Target."

"Ah. Well. Ready for me?"

"Right this way."

The kitchen stood empty for thirty seconds until Nanette appeared in the window on the door. She mouthed the word *typical* and then let herself inside. She took to the pantry and the cabinets. Now that she was a bit of a veteran in the prowling about strange kitchens, she knew how long to spend on each space. The trick for her was to not let the speed at which she opened the door affect how she closed it. One false slam and the whole operation would be compromised.

Meanwhile, Misses Dodd presented her honorable home to Rich. She talked about the honors her kids received in school and the work her husband put into redoing the bathroom tile and how the family has finally come back from the car accident six months ago which was an absolute tragedy not just for their minivan but for the girls, too. (*You know, Misses Dodd whispered in Rich's ear, that's why we had to move Virginia to the bottom bunk*). She'd gone through all the presentable areas of the home except for her garden. Misses Dodd, aside to her girls, said, "Go make Mister Rich a box of eggplant parm he can take home with him." And they scuttled off, their brother Roland taking the opportunity to hide from company in his room.

Misses Dodd led Rich by the arm out the back door into the garden where she showed him all her little rows of vegetables. There was a row for zucchini, for eggplant, and for cucumber. There was another for okra but Rich didn't know that vegetable by sight. A humble sprinkler glazed the vegetables with tiny iridescent beads, twinkling in the afternoon sun. He gazed upon the lush, verdant yard that was uncluttered by toy trucks. And then he saw the flowers. Daisies and dahlias and marigolds, lovely, each one was absolutely lovely. Someday, he thought. Then Rich asked if Emmalee did this all by herself, to which she said no. Mister Dodd liked to help out as much as he can, and when the kids weren't occupied with some activity then they too would lend a hand with the harvest. Misses Dodd tugged at Rich's elbow and said that the girls had something for him in the kitchen.

Though, in the kitchen, as Nanette had been finishing up her most thorough investigation yet, two extraneous variables barreled through the door. Just to make the reality that she didn't find her lunchbox in yet another house hurt more, she just had to go and get caught. Serves her right for thinking Richard could keep them distracted.

"Miss Nanette?" said the one with both feet.

"You did not see me here today, girl."

"Like a robber?"

"No! Not like a robber, what do you take me for?"

"More like a spy," said the other one.

"Sure, fine. More like a spy. I cannot be seen. So keep your mouths shut while I make my escape."

Nanette started for the door to outside when she was stopped short by one of the little girls' words.

"You can't go that way!"

"Why not?"

"Mama and Mister Rich are out there! You can't be seen."

"I think I will manage."

But as she said that she heard the returning voices of the other grownups.

Zola then jumped in her place and said, "V, make the plate for Mister Rich. Miss Nanette, over here."

"What? Don't touch me—" Zola took Nanette by the hand and paged the tablecloth for the long table they only ate dinner at. She ushered Nanette under and then dropped the cloth by the time Mama and Mister Rich came back inside.

"Girls?" said Mama, "You have that plate for Mister Rich?"

Rich scanned the kitchen, as if expecting something to be there. He glanced out the front window to his car, but turned away unsatisfied.

"Right here, Mama," said Virginia walking over to present Rich a plate with of eggplant parm covered with plastic wrap.

"Thank you, baby," said Misses Dodd handing the plate over to Rich. "Now I'll trust you to tell me if it's any good, now."

"Oh I will," Rich chuckled, and then chuckled again—less comfortable this time.

Virginia then locked eyes with Zola, who then gestured to the table. Virginia, understanding what her sister needed, grabbed onto Rich's side and yelled, "Ow! Ow! Ow!" She played up what she thought pain looked like.

Misses Dodd, recognizing her daughter's plea for attention, asked, "What's wrong, baby?"

"My ankle! Ow! My ankle hurts."

"Does it." Misses Dodd kneeled down to face Virginia. "Which one?"

"This one!" Virginia pointed to her prosthetic foot.

"Oh, well that looks pretty rough, doesn't it, Mister

Rich?"

Rich leaned forward to examine the girl's leg. "Oh, definitely."

With both grownups staring at Virginia's foot, Zola lifted up the tablecloth and waved Nanette through. The grown woman scrambled to her feet and then followed the little girl out through the back door of the kitchen. After the escape, Virginia quieted down.

"Baby," Misses Dodd said, "can't this wait until after Mister Rich leaves?"

"Yes it can," she admitted and then followed out where Zola and Miss Nanette had gone.

Zola, Virginia, and Nanette stood right outside the backdoor. Nanette was shuffling in place, raring to get back to the car. She sized up the wide-eyed girls before her.

Clearing her throat, Nanette said, "You did well. Could have done it on my own, but you did well."

"It's okay to need help," Zola offered. This, Nanette thought, was not untrue.

"But it's also okay to leave things be sometimes," Virginia said. This, Nanette thought, was just regular true.

She nodded goodbye to the girls, who waved as they watched her hop the fence. When Nanette got back to the car she couldn't help but notice that it smelled a lot like eggplant parmesan and that Rich's face was in his hands.

CHAPTER NINE

A BIRTHDAY PARTY

Nanette was driving back without the radio playing and without conversation. When Rich had finally taken his face out of his palms, he leaned his head back, staring, unmoving, at the ceiling of the car in a muted agony. What they had just done was messy and unrehearsed and he was surprised that they got out of there unseen by anybody. *It was gross*, he thought, *how simple it all seemed to search someone's house and abuse their kindness all because of one woman's neurotic impulses.*

All that said, it was a lovely day outside.

They were about a couple streets away from the house when Rich asked Nanette to stop the car. He unlocked his door and told Nanette that he would just walk from there.

"That work was satisfactory," Nanette said as he left.

"Yeah," Rich obliged. He pulled himself out of the car without looking back at her. The leftover eggplant parmesan from Misses Dodd was in his hands. Nanette's grip tightened around the wheel. Her unengaged foot bounced against the car floor. "Later." Rich went to shut his door.

"Richard," Nanette said, halting him, "is it business formal?"

"Eh?"

"The dress code. Is it business formal?"

"The dress code for what?" He was impatient.

"This birthday party for your great uncle."

"My sister."

"Right, right, your sister."

"You're going?" Rich turned to her with a tilt of his head and a release of his shoulders.

"I suppose I would if I knew the dress code. Is it business formal?"

"What? No. It's a birthday party. Casual. Not like a slob, but casual."

"Is there any way to change it to business formal? I may only have clothes that match that description."

"Nanette," he said, as he shut the car door.

It was unlike Rich to not tell Joey where he was heading. Joey mulled over this fact too many times for it to be healthy as he attempted to relax in the empty (often never empty) house. He mindlessly sat watching HGTV and yearning for the images he saw on the screen. Sprawled across the couch, Joey tapped his foot against one of the cushions, trying to get comfortable.

It wasn't that Rich and Joey didn't have secrets from each other—of course they did. It's impossible to fully know another human being. Trying to figure one's self out is challenging enough. But it had been so long since one of them went out to the store without so much as a quick update. Unless it was for a birthday present, but neither of their birthdays were close by. Joey thought he was ridiculous for being so worried. It was probably that Nanette's newer habits were just unsettling him. Hell, everyone in the house was a little unsettled.

But maybe it was him. Joey knew he wasn't the fastest person around. He didn't take a lot of initiative. He was consistent though, reliable. His cool-headedness was one of the reasons his relationship worked, to combat Rich's emotional bounds. Unless, in this case, it was working against him. Was he too slow? Was he getting there?

The garage door prattled open. Joey rushed to meet Nanette in the kitchen. To his surprise he found her without any grocery bags in her arms that he could help bring in.

"You didn't go grocery shopping?" he asked, a little disheartened.

"What? Oh, no, Joseph, no. I will be having the groceries delivered. I have decided that it is a noble profession and thought I would give them a fourth chance." Nanette started for the hallway. "Are overalls 'casual'?"

"What?"

"Never mind."

"Have you seen Rich?" Joey asked.

She slowed down. After a tick, "No. I should think not. Really, Joseph, I believe keeping track of Richard is a part of your, uh, department."

They awkwardly left through the same exit. Nanette retired to her bedroom, as was her weekend custom. Rich used to joke that she would pull an extension cord out of her ass and plug it in to recharge for the coming week. Joey had laughed, but interestingly enough he didn't dismiss it from the truth. Joey went back to watching television—but what that entailed was him watching the ceiling as the electric background noise filled the space.

After a while, he heard a door in the kitchen open.

Joey found Rich closing the refrigerator door. They exchanged heys and a welcoming peck. Rich's eyes wouldn't meet Joey's and fell short at his chest. Joey asked him if everything was okay.

"Yeah, uh, I just went for a walk. Needed some air. Crazy morning what with your grandmother showing up and all."

"You okay? If you want we can lie down, take a nap."

"Yeah, sounds good. A nap sounds good. I'll get a head start."

Joey lingered. He watched as Rich left and, when he was once again alone, opened up the fridge. There was a plate of eggplant parmesan wrapped up on a dish that Joey had never seen before. He felt his chest clench, but he couldn't comprehend why exactly. Turning off the television, Joey plunged the home into the ambient sounds of summertime and, alone, descended the stairs.

He knew that wherever Rich went, it wasn't just a walk. And if it wasn't just a walk, then why would he need to lie about it? Was Joey the only one in the household not wise to the ways of secret keeping? Joey reached his hand into his pocket and felt the fuzzy exterior the ring box and felt an undeniable burn of doubt. Of what? He wasn't sure. Doubting doubt itself.

And so, Joey played his part. He crawled down to their dungeon lair where his partner was already half-asleep on top of the covers. He pulled himself right up beside the sleeper and wondered to himself how long does a walk need to be to tucker a fit man out so completely? He traced the ridge of Rich's ear thinking to himself, *Sleep tight*, Richard Eliot, *sleep tight.*

The following day, a little after lunchtime, Joey found that the groceries had yet to be replenished and that the home was awfully quiet.

A bouquet of pale purple and yellow balloons bounced in the wind, tied to the banister of Cass Eliot's front porch. It was a big, old house with all the modern allowances of ventilation, insulation, and Wi-Fi. The house itself was atwitter with the comings of the Eliot family and the stampeding collection of friends Dorie had accumulated in her four years of high school.

The gruff, craggy-faced old men and their younger spouses—tight women, either with eyes for business or eyes for baked goods—populated the kitchen, dining and living areas of the first floor. Every few minutes, Cass would break away to give someone a tour of the bar he had built to look like a rustic Irish pub. The family sat around the food and grumbled about the things their legs used to be able to do, or discussed how pleasant days are at the paper factory. Old Mister Eliot sat in the living room, sunk into Cass's leather armchair by the fireplace. He wished that there would have been a fire lit for a little atmosphere, but Cass kept pointing out that it was the afternoon, in summer, with a house full of heat-producing human beings.

Out in the back was where one could find Dorie Eliot and her township of friends. Cass was never so popular. Part of Cass resented his little sister for her social success. But he needed to remind himself that nothing she did was a threat to him, as he was the one in charge of the paper factory and that he was a planned baby. Old Mister Eliot assured Dorie that she was no accident, even though it was dubious why the Eliots were compelled for a final child twelve years after the birth of their first.

The day was an example of how summer was beautiful and how the weather could have other plans. The sunlight shone on the home, most likely burning some of Dorie's pastier compatriots. Loitering at the sky's horizon was a line of clouds though that was bound to make Cass skeptical. He didn't recall how he was in charge of setting up Dorie's eighteenth but he took it to remind her that this was her last big birthday—she'd be taking care of the rest.

Trudging up the front porch, him in his usual garb and her in dusty overalls and a borrowed T-shirt, came Rich Eliot and his date, Nanette. They each held a present. Nanette's was a rectangular prism wrapped so tightly that it looked as if the present was suffocating. Rich held a tiny metallic bag with both a Starbucks and an Amazon gift card inside.

"I still can't believe you wore that," Rich groaned.

"It's casual, Richard. I do not know what else to tell you."

"Do you remember the plan?"

"We are going to cheat your treacherous family into trusting you once more in order to usurp their hard-earned paper money."

"What? No. I want to talk to them. That's all."

"Yes, well, okay. I will in the meantime go along with believing that you believe that."

"And remember, you're my date. You shouldn't have to lie that much about our history."

"What if someone asks me if you have intercourse with other men?"

Rich sighed. "It's a birthday party, Nanette. You've been to a birthday party before."

Nanette thought back to the hand puppet fiasco of 2006 and shuddered.

"Yes," she said, "I have."

Rich entered his brother's home and the reaction was not at all what he had expected. He envisioned a hush to fall and the only audible things would be a running faucet that his mother was frozen at washing dishes and a playlist of songs from the early 2000s. The people would be exchanging looks, uncomfortably, knowingly. Instead, the chatter continued. It was the white noise of festivities, and though it began to hush—an eventual *Rich* entered the air from a number of different voices—there was no Earth-stopping moment.

His father wasn't in sight, which was why he was still in the house.

But after the thrill of crossing borders, Rich remembered, or started remembering, the faces that had sat back when Rich was forced to disappear. Aunts, who had married in, thinking themselves invisible, were scampering out of the room as if to warn their husbands. He saw the faces he hadn't for two years aged slightly, or if he'd seen them on Facebook he saw them at their real angles, unfiltered and less flattering. He felt no warmth in their expressions. Though, he felt no hatred either. Pity. He felt their pity. They had sided with the power and with the money and not with the boy whose refuge was his boyfriend and a woman whose idea of casual was a pair of overalls.

"Rich," Cass appeared with a drink in his hand, "you showed up."

"I was invited."

"I know, I invited you. Who is this?"

"This is my, uh, date, Nanette," Rich presented. Nanette did not move when Cass went to shake her hand.

"Hi, Nanette, I'm Cass Eliot. Rich's brother."

"Oh, are you?" Nanette began. "I could not have possibly figured that out from the conversation you—"

"—Nanette is," Rich interjected, "forward thinking. And forward speaking. Sometimes she forgets how to meet new people because she thinks we all know each other already."

"That's a little weird," Cass admitted. To Nanette he asked, "That true?"

"I feel inclined to say yes."

Cass coughed. Then he said, "You want to see Dorie?"

Rich perked up and nodded. Cass ushered him and Nanette through the house. Nanette saw walls of framed photographs with several empty, faded areas and exposed hooks. There were portraits that failed to fully cover some other discolored patches on the walls. She listened in to snippets of conversations between business friends, family friends, muted disputes between couples. She could scarcely tell it was a birthday party.

Until, at least, she got outside.

There were tent canopies set up over buffets filled with pastas, curries, sushi, a make-your-own taco station, and a make-your-own sundae bar. There were platters of dessert foods *and* finger foods. Platters of deli meats and cheeses. Platters of fruits and vegetables. Way more food than the party quite frankly needed. There was an in-ground pool packed with teenagers. The whole graduating class must have been out there either on the patio or jumping into the deep end.

"She's out here somewhere," Cass said. "You want I should tell Pa you're here?"

"No," said Rich. "I'll greet him myself, thank you."

"Alright, you know where to find me." He then grinned at Nanette, nodded, and headed inside. She had a smart mouth, Cass thought, but at least she was pretty.

Rich reached for Nanette's arm but she pulled it away. She refused to be led even if she didn't know what they were looking for while wading through this swamp of teenagers. The couple ended up near the corner of a buffet tent with Rich on his tiptoes searching for his sister. Usually when they went out in big groups, Rich didn't have to worry about finding someone because Joey was just tall enough to take care of all that.

"Rich?" said a young voice behind them.

"Dorie!" Rich cried with overbearing enthusiasm.

There was a girl in a two-piece bathing suit, almost as tall as Rich, and with her hair pulled back. The two nearly strangled each other in an embrace until after a minute or so when the girl stepped back and noticed Nanette. Her eyes widened.

"Let me introduce," Rich stammered. "Nanette, this is my little sister Dorie. Dorie, this is my date, Nanette."

"A pleasure," Dorie said.

"I am sure," Nanette replied.

Dorie turned back to Rich and said, "Your date?"

"Yes."

"Mhmm," the girl smirked. "I didn't expect to see you!"

"Cass invited me."

"Cass invited you? Why would he do that?"

"I called him the other day."

"You called Cass before you would call me?"

"I'm here, aren't I? Here, take this."

Rich handed her his gift and she thanked him. Then, when Rich recalled that Nanette had a gift for Dorie as well, he said that she should open it. Nanette handed over the present and Dorie graciously tore it open. When the paper shell was on the ground, Dorie looked at the gift with a slightly open mouth without words coming out. Rich sidled beside Dorie to see.

"A GRE prep book?" Rich was incredulous.

"It was mine," Nanette said. "You said she was going to school."

"She's eighteen, Nanette."

"It's cool," Dorie said, "It'll be super useful. Eventually, I mean."

Dorie rejoined her friends, and so Rich decided it was time to try and assimilate back into family life. He and Nanette returned inside and tried to find someone to talk to. With certainty, Nanette often voiced her desire to return home and reminded Rich of the good fortune she was providing for him, to which Rich would reply that she was a mad would-be burglar who spends her free time invading the homes of children and, well, there was a bit of a damper on the conversation after that.

Neither Rich nor Nanette could bring themselves to eat anything, but every time the two ran into someone that did not know what to say they would ask if the couple had anything to eat. To which they always said yes.

Until, "Richard?"

Nanette turned to see a short, frail woman. She would have pegged her to be about a couple of decades or so younger than Grandmother but that would mean that Grandmother was born instead of a demon who crawled up from hell before the invention of time.

"Ma?" Rich said. It looked like he was readying a hug.

"What are you doing here?"

"What?"

She kept wringing a dish towel in her hands even though it was almost completely dry.

"What are you doing here?" she repeated.

"It's Dorie's birthday."

"But you know how your father is…"

"I can't celebrate my sister's birthday?"

Rich's mother looked away, and then at Nanette. "Who is this cowgirl?"

"This cowgirl," Nanette sneered, "is called Nanette. You can tell by all the cattle I tracked into the home with me. Oh, wait? Where are they? I must have left them in a reasonable location like a ranch. Or the wild west."

"Well, hello, Nanette," she said weakly.

"The dress code is casual."

Rich stepped in. "This is my date, Ma."

"Oh? I thought—well, isn't that nice."

"It's okay."

"How did you two meet?"

"A mutual friend," Rich said.

"Who?"

"You wouldn't know him."

"What?" Nanette voiced. "You probably know of him, Misses Eliot. Given the amount of time they spent together in college"—she met Rich's belligerent gaze—"but now that I am thinking about it, it, it might be likely that he is a complete foreigner to you because . . . because he is a foreigner. He lived in the Amazon."

"The Amazon," Rich repeated. It sounded like he was in pain.

"How… exciting," Misses Eliot said. "Did you tell me your whole name?"

"Nanette Abbot—"

Rich went to say no, but it came out as: "Nnnnnnn Costello. Costello."

"Abbot-n-Costello?" Misses Eliot said, unimpressed.

"Just Costello," Rich said. "Nanette Costello. She just likes to say Abbot to confuse people, like one of their old bits. Right, dear?"

Nanette blinked.

"Haha," Rich grasped. "Third base!"

"What are you even talking about, Rich?" Nanette asked.

Rich shook his head, and to his mother he said, "Such a kidder."

The name Abbot was well known in the Eliot household because of how Joey and Rich were best friends all throughout college. Joey was a welcomed face in the Eliot homes up until they found out that the nature of the relationship was more intimate than previously assumed.

Rich then felt somebody grab him by the back of his shirt and pull him away from the conversation.

Old Mister Eliot told everyone to get out of Cass's new bar in the renovated basement. It was a passion project that took Cass several years to complete, just in time for them to decide to move out. Old Mister Eliot dragged Rich inside, scuffing up the dark wooden floors. Rich's brother Cass shut the bar's door behind them. The room itself was dimly lit. Only strip lights bordering the ceiling were turned on. The walls were painted with Celtic designs and made to look like they were cracked in certain places.

The father pushed Rich away, giving him some room to regain his footing.

"What was that for—?"

Old Mister Eliot cut Rich off, "What are you doing here? Forever used to mean a lot longer than two years." He also bore the thick local accent sported by his eldest son.

"Pa, I—"

"I don't wanna hear it, Richard. You're going to collect whatever it is you brought with you and you're going to leave. Do I make myself clear?"

"I wanted to see you."

"Bullshit."

"I wanted to see Dorie, at least."

Cass interjected, "Pa, he should at least be able to see his sister."

"Shut up, Cass. Shut the hell up. And for you," Old Mister said, pointing a finger at Rich, "I don't want you talkin' to your sister. I don't want you messin' with her. You're to leave her alone—not until you get bored or you're too weak and can't make it on your own."

"Jesus Christ, Pa," Cass muttered.

"Shut up, Cass. Ya knew it was like this. Everyone knew, and everyone was okay. Richard, get out. Go."

"I've changed, Pa," Rich mustered.

"Bullshit."

"It's true," Cass vouched, "he brought a date."

"I'm not interested in your flower boys, Rich."

"It's a woman," Cass clarified.

"Bullshit."

"It's true," Rich said. "You pulled me away from her. I don't even know what she's doing now."

Nanette was recruited by some of Dorie's more inquisitive friends. All girls. She sat on the end of a lounge chair by the pool. A blonde, sipping a virgin piña colada, asked her, "Are the rumors about Dorie's brother true?"

"Rumors?" Nanette asked.

"You know, does he… you know… sleep with other guys?"

Nanette sighed. "I cannot confirm nor deny."

The group giggled.

"She can't make it out there by herself," Rich said.

"Then you better get going," Old Mister Eliot spat.

"You can't do this. I'm your son."

"Cass is my son, too. Cass never disgraced the family. I don't know who in the hell you brought with you today but I know you're too stubborn to just switch like that. So you're going to go."

Old Mister Eliot walked to the bar's closed exit. Cass moved out of his way.

"You're a terrible person," Rich said.

"Hmm?" Old Mister Eliot turned.

"You are a terrible person. You're supposed to love your family, and you threw me out. How could you do that? I had nowhere to go. I spent weeks in limbo just trying to find someplace quiet to stand. And you did that."

"And Jesus wept," said Old Mister Eliot. And then he left.

Neither brother spoke.

Until, "Jesus, Rich."

And then Cass left too.

Rich watched as a slow drop of water fell at his feet. He felt the phantom move his arm and wipe his face. He sucked in, found Nanette, and went home.

When they got there, Joey, reddened face, didn't have time to
ask where they'd gone before Rich was in his arms.

CHAPTER TEN

JON FLETCHER

Jon Fletcher was the oldest, and therefore the wisest, of the ten children in Baby Badger. However, Jon's soft personality kept other kids from approaching him to ask questions, seek advice, and the like. His power among the kids was unspoken, unsung, and assumed. So rather than making a show of his dominance, like the kids at school would have done to establish the difference between the haves and the have-nots, Jon kept to himself mostly. Except for those moments he sought out someone to play with, in which case he approached Roux and her little ones.

Monday morning, though there was no rain, the clouds covered the sky and the kids were, for safety's sake, stuck inside to play. The struggle was that Mister Joey and Mister Rich didn't have anything else to do like an arts and crafts project or a baking activity. Oddly enough, groceries were being delivered to the house right now and the kids all had to play downstairs in the playroom until one of the grownups came to collect them.

Jon was listening in on the seven-year-olds playing spies like they had all last week. The goal was for one of them to make it from the playroom to the bathroom without the other two noticing.

Javier kept losing the game, unable to stay out of sight from Figgy and Meadow. And because he kept losing, it kept being his turn. Jon couldn't help him because he didn't know the exact rules of the game. All he knew was that Javier failed try after try attempting to bypass his friends. The one rule that seemed evident was that every failure was followed by Meadow or Figgy saying: Loser plays Miss Nanette. Javier must have been Miss Nanette for five rounds. It wasn't until Virginia stepped forward that something changed.

Virginia set aside her sketchbook. She felt like an expert in regards to being sneaky, so she approached the seven-year-olds with her head up. Jon watched Zola put down her own sketchbook in awe. The groups tended not to mesh this early in the day.

"You need to distract them," Virginia advised Javier.

"What do you know?" Meadow asked. She was next to play Miss Nanette and did not enjoy how hard it looked.

"Because it worked for us."

"V…" Zola got up and grabbed her sister by the arm. This information was power and she didn't think it wise to compromise that.

"You saw Miss Nanette, too?" Figgy asked, stepping forward.

"Yes. This weekend," Virginia boasted.

Meadow sunk her head.

Figgy said, "I thought it was just me and Javy."

"Oh that's just great," Meadow groaned.

"And we had to make a distraction to keep her hidden. We were spies," Virginia voiced despite Zola tugging on her arm.

"Yeah okay," said Meadow. "We want to get back to the game."

"Is there anyone else?" Figgy asked. "Who saw Miss Nanette? Anyone else who might want to play with us?"

"Fig…" went Meadow.

It was quiet after that for a spell. Then Pax, all the way

from the corner, shouted, "Yeah, Yuki saw her too."

"Really?" Figgy smiled. "Do you guys want to play with us? Who wants to be Miss Nanette?"

They were so entangled in the discussion that only Jon noticed when Mister Joey entered the room. He wasn't very engaged in the Badgers' conversation but knew enough to ask them about it.

"What's all this about Miss Nanette?" Joey chuckled. He imagined what kind of a character she must have been to these kids.

"It's a game," Figgy said.

"I'm sure. Lunch will be ready soon. Anyone who wants to help is welcome."

When he was gone, the kids went back to playing for the duration of the morning. The seven-year-olds invited Virginia and Zola to play with them. They tried to even out the teams a bit more. There was the idea of adding a second Miss Nanette to have two people trying to get to one place at the same time. Virginia didn't bring it up to the other kids that Mister Rich was also at their house but that was because, for all she knew, Mister Rich had no clue that Miss Nanette was there at all. Jon noticed shortly that Meadow kept adding rules to the game that worked against the twins' success. The littler girls didn't realize it, but by the time Jon or Figgy would have gone to say something about it, it was time to eat.

The plan for today was set. Nanette was to return home at her usual time. She would come in, say hello as casually as she could muster, and say she forgot something or come up with some reason to leave the house again. Then Rich would meet her and they would be off to the next child's home. As much as it vexed her, Nanette had to admit that Rich's assistance in the Dodd job not only provided a thorough investigation but also kept the search from slowing down an entire weekend. She thought about the boys' false desire to move away. Nanette almost laughed at the prospect of the boys picking up and attempting to make it on their own. They were just children. Blind teenagers, lost in the world. They needed Nanette even if it meant that she had to sacrifice her peace, her solitude, her calm.

They needed her and she was the only one capable, and culpable to help them out.

As she pulled into her driveway, glancing at the neighborhood turtle out of the corner of her eye, her phone rang.

"Nanette," Nanette said.

"Hello dearie, it's Grandmother."

"How do you have my number?"

"Is beige still your favorite color?"

"I do not want a new lunchbox, Grandmother."

She didn't need another excuse to stop by the house again. Nanette thought this as the car pulled into the garage.

"I know how you hate those brown paper bags."

"Don't," Nanette's voice cracked.

"Joseph told me that he and Richard might be looking for their own place. Isn't that nice?"

"You're a monster."

"I didn't tell them. I thought you did."

"You deluded bag. Of course, I would not have told them."

"Well you should. I would think that somebody ought to—"

Nanette hung up.

This was what Grandmother did. She poisoned the mind, drudged up sunken memories from the polluted riverbed of repression. Nanette went months without thinking back to what she had said. She hadn't done anything to Joey, regardless of her Grandmother's virulent accusations. Nanette never thought that she ever obsessed over anything that didn't need obsessing over. It was her Grandmother, that stone thrower, that wave maker, who was the epicenter of her grief. And what was worse was that Nanette was the only one who could see it, because if Joey saw it then who was to say who the real monster was?

Even now, as she sat in the garage, Nanette was burying the thought. Joey, and even Rich, couldn't know what the reason was why she took them in. Guilt? No, she had never known how guilt manifested in the body. By this time Nanette thought that guilt was a made-up emotion designed to make her guess herself. Then, if it wasn't guilt, could it have been … family? That concept of loving another, as Nanette turned it around in her head, was almost as misguided as feeling guilty. Nanette had only ever needed and known herself. Maybe the point now was that more people needed her too, now. They needed her. But they were too naïve to know that. Yes, yes, let's go with that. Let's go with that.

Rich got into the car then. Nanette jumped at the click of the handle.

"I was supposed to come inside," she declared.

"I want to get this over with," he said. "You ready to go?"

Regular old Nanette replied, "No, Richard. I just left the engine running because I thought we could have a nice chat."

And then they pulled out of the house.

Joey called Rich's name. There wasn't a response. He resolved to carry on with some cleaning. In the sink, Joey found the unfamiliar plate that Rich had brought home. The alien eggplant parm was gone, and Joey was expected to clean up after it. Slowly, methodically, he grabbed the plate. His thumb pressed into the tomato sauce on the rim. It was cold and unsettling and made his hand crimson. Joey thought that Nanette was inside his arm. He carried the plate over to the garbage, and threw it away.

"Now that hardly seems like the solution here," he said, but the house, he knew, was empty.

Marianne Fletcher was trying to redefine herself as the woman who could have it all. And she was succeeding. She divorced her husband about three years prior and has only been on the rise since. She worked part-time at a local grocer to help with the rent while her startup company was still finding its feet. She used to work in manuscript acquisitions but decided that she should make her own publishing house to produce the stories that she liked the most. She has since reached out to other book lovers in her circle to give her a hand, such as Tsukuru Green and his love for Young Adult novels. Starting this year, Marianne Fletcher was no longer operating on a loss. The biggest thing she had to contend with was helping pay for her daughter's college tuition seeing how she'd be entering her sophomore year in the coming fall.

After she kicked her deadbeat husband out, she reveled in proving wrong all the people who said she would need help. And it was true that she needed help, but she only accepted it from people who believed that she could make it without them. Like that Joey Abbot. He was one of the nicest guys, offering to look after her Jon like that. Joey was such an easygoing person that she could trust him with just about anything (and considering the goods and services she got from him over the years, she knew that this was undeniable).

So now she kept her hair cropped at her shoulders and took up jogging in the mornings right before the start of her eleven-hour workdays and profusely thanked her daughter for when she could pick Jon up from the Baby Badger Cub Club. She knew that Jon was on the older side for daycare so she tried to view it as a summer camp. Plus, Jon liked it there. If he hated it at Joey's then she would find somewhere else for Jon to spend his summer but this arrangement was just so convenient.

Not to mention she liked giving business to Joey and Rich. Ever since she came to terms with her own bisexuality she felt a certain kinship with those boys that she never properly articulated nor did they fully reciprocate. Not that she had a lot of time to think about these matters. Marianne Fletcher's phone had the nasty habit of receiving a phone call every ten seconds—an exaggeration that she wished was only an exaggeration.

Marianne was on the phone with one of her new employees. She had let Jon watch television in the other room.

She used to think that TV rotted the mind, but then she realized he couldn't sit quietly without being bored forever. He got his one hour every day, and then the rest needed to be books. He was on one of those *Percy Jackson* spinoff series but Marianne didn't have the time to figure out which one. She couldn't wait until she had time again to read alongside him. It was coming soon, she told herself.

Nanette and Rich pulled up to the Fletcher residence. After the divorce, Marianne found a lovely duplex that one of her mother's ex-girlfriends lived in the upper half of. The breakup was amicable so the home was available. Or so Rich had been told, at least.

The plan was more or less the same as the Dodd job. As a reminder: the plan for the Dodd job was for Rich to go in and for Rich to look around the kitchen. That just wasn't Nanette's intention. Nanette, though debatable if she was listening or not, felt the need to let Rich say whatever he believed the plan was. If he didn't understand that he couldn't be trusted to complete the investigation on his own then that was his problem. But, if he needed an agreement that she would stay in the car, then she would ostensibly acquiesce.

So Rich got out of the car and walked up the steps to the Fletcher home. He carried with him Jon's cardigan that he had hidden earlier in the day for an excuse to drop in. Nanette watched as a woman only a couple years older than herself opened the door and welcomed Rich with a smile and a speedy embrace. Nanette also noticed how people seemed to like Rich. She supposed people liked Joey too. She wondered what it took.

As soon as she saw Rich be ushered inside, Nanette hopped out of the car and ran around to the back of the house. It was much more overgrown than the front. The greenery only grew in patches, many of which were just heads of crabgrass. So much of the yard was dirt that it made Nanette wish she wore her Thursday shoes, a detail completely incapable to being understood for anyone outside of Nanette's head. Lining the back of the house and the nearby fences were shrubs and bushes all with different intensities of decay. Some were still lush and green while others were just brown skeletons of plants.

There was a window to peer inside the home accessible from the ground. The trouble was that there was a bush that butted up against the house tightly, with little regard to the house's personal space. Nanette understood the need for sacrifice and, even though she might damage her suit, wriggled her way between the house and the bush. She felt the invasive pokes of the bush's protrusions digging into her back. Twigs snapped off as she moved and fell away in tandem with her grunts.

"The trick is to come in from the other side."

Nanette jumped. The voice was new and entirely unexpected in this location.

"Who in the heck are you?" Nanette felt weak in her constitutions for swearing but she was caught off guard by the sight of a bearded man, in an ill-fitting suit, also hiding in the bush with her.

"Um. Samson," he said.

"Um Samson?"

"Just Samson. The 'um' was an accident."

"And what, pray tell, are you doing in this bush?"

"I'm doing what you're doing," Samson said. "What are you doing?"

"That is not, nor will ever be, your business, Um Samson."

"Well that puts us in an odd situation, doesn't it?"

"Are you peeping on this poor, unknowing family?"

"Is that what you're doing?"

"I am performing reconnaissance."

"On Annie? She finally get herself mixed up with the wrong people?"

"Get out of this bush!"

"I was here first."

"I was here second. Do we want to go around listing facts now?"

"No, no."

"Leave."

"Or what?"

"I could scream."

Samson narrowed his gaze at Nanette and said, "You wouldn't dare jeopardize your mission."

Nanette sighed. Then she took in a gulp of air and an instant before any kind of shout, Samson cupped his hand over her mouth. To which she punched him in the stomach. And as they both reeled from the event, Samson spoke.

"Okay, okay, I'm just checking up on my family."

"And you are doing so from the shadows? Ah! No, you are stalking this poor, unknowing family."

"It's my family!"

"I can tell. You know, what with the fact that you are spending such quality time with them from the comfort of a shrubbery."

"You're spying too."

"Something was taken from me."

"And you're just going to take it back? That's stealing."

"Reclaiming. And you do not know anything about my situation. You, sir, are morally abject. Think of this invasion of privacy. This, this, mockery of care."

"And you are so high and mighty, Misses…"

"Miss."

"Miss what?"

"Miss your chance to figure out my name. Rookie mistake, Um Samson. You are a creep and are done here."

"Don't act like you're in any better shape than I am."

"Please. If anything you have way more at stake than I do. I might just be a small-time burglar. I am not, because I am not morally abject, but you do not know that."

Nanette realized that she was losing time when the hushed emanations of a television went silent and the living room on the other side of the window became empty. Fighting against the cramped space, she squirmed her way back out from behind the bush. She couldn't get far before Samson grabbed her wrist, impeding her exit.

"Where are you going?" he queried.

"Now is my chance."

"You're not going in there?"

"I am. Out of my way, you sad, sad little man."

Nanette was stronger than Samson, so rather than him pulling her back behind the bush, she tore him out into the open. Every few seconds, Nanette would look over her shoulder into the house, afraid to catch sight of Rich bungling the operation. Then she realized that Samson had placed himself between her and the door. She faked left to get by him but he managed to counter her. Nanette's eye twitched as she raised her fists. Samson's fingers fidgeted as he put up his own dukes to meet hers.

"You don't want to do this," Samson advised.

"You know what? I just adore it when people tell me what it is that I do and do not want. Because more often than not, they always are so close to being right. I have always valued other people's opinions."

As they spoke, they circled each other. The unlikely sparrers rounded the dirt yard like it was a boxing ring. By the time either one of them was willing to throw an untrained punch, it was pointless. Samson and Nanette had circled the yard so much that he wasn't standing between her and the door anymore. She broke away as Samson lunged. He fell, face in the muck, advising her one last time not to go in.

Nanette spat, and said, "You are weak and will not survive the winter."

Samson found this to be true, and strangely ominous seeing how it was a lovely summer eve.

After entering, Nanette noticed three things about the room: the dark screen of the television, the plush and neatly vacuumed state of the carpet, and the child on the sofa looking over the cover of a novel at her. Her shoulders slumped at the sight of the boy.

"The television is off. This room was supposed to be empty."

"I'm reading," Jon replied, afraid to contest her. "I went to get my book, Miss Nanette."

"Alright. But keep your mouth shut."

"I don't usually read with my mouth open."

Nanette cracked her knuckles. Jon went back to his book. Nanette thought that his rapport with her was odd. He held himself as if he was expecting her—but how could that have remotely been possible?

She sized up the room: there were three main exits. One led to the backyard where the depressing troll man lost his willpower (or whatever happened back there, Nanette wasn't really paying attention). Another was a hallway, most likely leading to the bedrooms and bathroom. There was one last one that, based on the layout of the home, led to the kitchen. Though she knew it wouldn't be in here, she performed a quick sweep of the current room for the lunchbox before heading to the kitchen door.

"Wait!" Jon urged as Nanette reached for the knob. She shushed him.

Jon knew that his mother and Mister Rich were still in there. All the other kids at Baby Badger kept Miss Nanette safe (more or less). Zola and Virginia probably kept her safe. Figgy and Javier didn't get her in trouble. Jon wondered if the kids knew that Nanette could get in trouble. But he didn't want to be the kid to find out. He pushed his book aside and ran in between Nanette and the door.

Nanette noted that this may have been a like-father-like-son scenario.

"Let me through, child," Nanette instructed.

But Jon replied only with, "Patience."

Jon liked the word patience because it was a huge help to him. He spent a lot of time alone, or waiting for his mom whom he loved and knew that if she could then she would be right there next to him. He'd taken to waiting, which was something Nanette didn't know she was deficient in.

Through the door, Jon heard Mister Rich: "Thank you for being so understanding, Marianne."

"You're welcome, Rich! I'll ask Jon but the lunchbox isn't in the kitchen so I don't know if you'll find it here."

"He sold me down the river," Nanette gasped. "He was not to tell her of my lunchbox. The mission's compromised."

"Do you mind if I use your bathroom?"

"Of course, it's this way."

Jon, understanding the immediacy of Miss Nanette's condition, ran to the back door and threw it open. He pointed through the aperture to get Miss Nanette outside. She then glanced at the open door, and then back to the closed kitchen door. She was afraid to do the unspeakable: trust Richard Eliot's word. If he had searched the kitchen, then he must have searched the kitchen. Even if he divulged classified information to the enemy.

As the knob began to rattle, Nanette ducked outside. Jon pulled it shut and leapt onto the sofa. He picked up his book upside down but didn't notice as the grownups came into the room.

"Hey, Jon," Mister Rich said.

"Hi!" Jon returned, acting engaged with his story.

Then, a bombastic gripe shouted from outside: "Aww nuts!"

It was a woman's voice. Rich and Marianne met eyes. Marianne said nervously, "There's someone outside."

And Rich, who was a different kind of nervous, said, "Sounds like it."

They rushed to the back door and battered into the yard.

Nanette held Samson Fletcher in a chokehold as he tried to scramble away. They scuffled in the dust until Marianne stepped forward.

"What is going on here?" she yelled.

"Annie!" Samson gasped.

"Is that your ex-husband?" Rich asked, horrified.

"Yes, it is," Marianne spoke, funereal in tone. Then she got Nanette's attention. "Ma'am? Ma'am who are you?"

"Crazy!" Samson offered.

"Who am I?" Nanette repeated. "I am… Detective."

"Detective," Marianne echoed.

"Detective… Grocery Store. Detective G. Store. We have reason to believe that this man has been stalking you for some time."

"Jesus Christ," said Rich.

"Really, Samson?" Marianne groaned. "How many people need to find you in these bushes before you can take a hint? I'd hate to have to get a restraining order against you."

"What?" Samson blurted. "She's lying!"

"You mean to tell me that you aren't hiding in my backyard?"

"Oh, come on."

"Ma'am," Nanette said, "would you like to press charges?"

"No," Marianne sighed, "just get him off my property."

"Alright. Have a good evening, ma'am."

Five minutes later, after Rich used the restroom and said goodbye to the Fletchers, he expected to see Samson at the car. Rich asked Nanette what she did with him.

"Let him go, with a warning," Nanette said.

"What?"

"I have bigger things to worry about than trolls." She clenched her fist, investigating her scratched up knuckles, and then released her grip. Exhaling, she had trouble remembering how the handle of her lunchbox used to feel in her palm.

Joey sat on the bed with the closet door open. He stared inside and wondered if he ever would get that real garden. He didn't like Rich not telling him where he went off to, whereas with Nanette he could understand a little bit more. Nanette was allowed her hiccups in personality because they'd been inevitable for quite some time. This wasn't regular Rich.

He listened as the rumbling of the garage door signified Nanette's return.

He also listened to the unlikely bickering that followed.

The sound carried an argument between Nanette and, it appeared to be, Rich. *Why did you wait the entire ride to bring it up in the garage?*

Is it so unlikely to just stay in the car?

Yes! I am being thorough.

I can't even look at you right now.

Joey followed the rumors of Rich stomping down the stairs until he appeared in the bedroom, fuming. Joey had anticipated Rich starting with a hello, or an explanation as to where he had been, but no. Rich, with a huff, muttered something about Nanette under his breath as he stripped off his sweater and plopped onto the bed.

"Were you out with Netty?" Joey asked.

"Huh? Oh, uh, no. I don't, I do not know where she was."

"Oh, okay. What were you arguing about?"

"Nothing important."

"If it wasn't important… can't you tell me?"

Rich hadn't the time to answer. Nanette barged into the bedroom in the middle of a sentence, "And another thing, Richard—"

"Nanette! Knocking? Maybe?" Richard sat up on the bed.

"Guys, come on," Joey tried but they drowned him out.

Rich kept yelling for a minute or so until they noticed Nanette staring off into the corner. Joey said first, "Nanette?"

"What is that?" Nanette said pointing to the open closet.

"Jesus Christ," Rich whispered as Joey got up to close the door. Nanette anticipated him and lunged across the room. She took a lesson from the Fletchers and put herself in between him and the door.

She looked over her shoulder. Joey watched the wrath drain from her face and be replaced by some form of advanced, super-wrath.

"What on Earth are you two doing in my house?!"

"Whoa, Netty," said Joey, "it's Massachusetts… Weed's barely illegal."

"Keep your head, Nanette," Rich advised.

"Keep. My. Head? Dear lord. Sure, why would I not keep my head? I should help usher in the new age of the Abbot opium den. The cannabis carnival. I open up my home to you boys when no one else would take you and let you turn it into a children's circus and this is the thanks I am so grateful to receive? What in everlasting heck! Today it is just a low-key marijuana operation in the basement and then tomorrow it is human trafficking. Probably enlisting all those children to help plow these fields. I work hard for all of our wellbeing out of my own selflessness and at the end of the day the house is still subject to police raid. You are just here having a laugh and growing doobies!"

"Oh my god, Joseph, she just said 'growing doobies.'"

"Nanette…" Joey trailed off.

"I should report you."

"To who?" Rich spat. "Detective Store?"

"Who?" Joey blurted.

"Watch yourself, Richard."

"You mean to tell me, Nanette," Rich sneered, "that you don't have your own secrets?"

"Rich, what are you doing?" Joey threw out there.

"Yes, watch yourself, Richard," Nanette warned.

"*Au contraire*," Rich said. "You aren't going to rat us out."

"And why shouldn't I?"

"Because," Rich got up to face her, and then he turned to Joey. "Nanette has been breaking into the houses of all the kids in the daycare!"

"What?" Joey stammered.

"All in pursuit of her stupid lunchbox!"

"It is not stupid, Richard! And tell me, how are you so privy to this information? This is a grand accusation."

"Because I've seen you!"

"Nanette, is this true?" Joey tried to understand.

"Yes, but Rich was with me! He, too, bears this cross! Besmirched by circumstance!"

"Yes, but I've just been visiting friends," Rich defended.

"You broke into homes! Trying to steal from young families."

"What the hell," Joey muttered.

"You have marijuana in your closet!"

"You have marijuana in your basement!"

"Wait," Joey stepped forward.

Nanette started, "You're an accomplice to breaking and entering!"

"An operation that you started!"

"Wait," Joey separated the two others.

"*Drug dealer!*" Nanette yelled.

"*Manic burglar!*"

"*Wait a second!*" Joey raised his voice. Both Rich and Nanette took a step back, keeping their eyes on Joey. He turned to Rich and asked, "You've been helping her break into the parents' houses these past few days? That's where you've been going?"

"Yes!" Nanette taunted.

Rich stared at the carpet. "Yes."

"Oh . . . that's great!" Joey clamped his arms around Rich and swung him around in a circle, laughing.

"What?" Nanette said.

Joey put Rich on the ground and, laughing, he said, "I thought you were cheating on me!"

"Don't be ridiculous, Joseph," Rich said. "Cheating on you? Oh, I'm so sorry."

"Jiminy cricket, Joseph," Nanette voiced, "Richard may be dubious company but he's no infidel."

"I'm sorry?" Joey said-asked.

"No, I'm sorry." Rich kissed his cheek.

"I am the sorriest of us all," Nanette felt necessary to add. "How long have you been growing cannabis in my home?"

"Forever," Joey sighed. "Longer than the daycare."

"Longer?"

"We started the daycare to help out the people we sold to. All the kids we know are from parents who buy from us."

"That is the most ludicrous thing I have ever heard."

Rich doubted that that was true but didn't feel the need to

point it out.

"Besides," Joey began, "we are stopping this. We're just going to be childcare professionals without a background in drug dealing."

"Well. . . " Nanette pondered this, "good. This is not over."

The three stood in the bedroom, changing glances. All Joey could hear was the burning of his scented candle. A minute must have passed until Joey finally spoke.

"Now what?"

CHAPTER ELEVEN

MEADOW DESCOTEAUX

It was Tuesday. They were now well enough into the second week since the vanishing of Nanette's lunchbox. All of her previous efforts had had fewer results than Nanette cared to admit. Even now, seeing as the members of the household kept all conversation brief and their eyes forward.

At lunchtime, Joey sat at his end of the table with the platoon of children between him and Rich. Joey watched over the kids, wondering which of their homes had been invaded by Nanette. They had told him that Rich had less to do with the searches for the godforsaken lunchbox, but it didn't make Joey feel any better. There was something unnerving about Rich and Nanette spending time with each other. Perhaps, Joey speculated, he was discomfited by the unlawful behavior executed without his knowledge. But perhaps, it was because Joey didn't like the idea of being discussed between the two people who, arguably, know him the best. He took a second to mourn—if Nanette Abbot was one of his best friends, then maybe he'd done something wrong. Like cut off a witch doctor in traffic, or tell those kids from UNICEF that his wallet was in a different jacket. He didn't know if he believed in karma, but he hoped that he'd led a respectable life up to this point.

Joey leaned back. He was coolheaded.

He examined the children at the table, laughing, trading bits of their meals with each other. There was something extra-communal about the kids today. Virginia was joking around with Figgy who passed some bread to Javier who was trying to talk to Yuki. Meadow poked her food around on her plate and then changed Figgy's conversation. Jon sat across from Roux who was cleaning something off of her brother's face, but he was leaning over to hear Zola's conversation with Yuki and Javier. The Tenth Child sat still, like he was made of stone. Joey couldn't tell if the Tenth Child was listening to anything or if the scuttlebutt was just breezing by him.

Joey was still fuzzy on the details with how Nanette could've enlisted Rich but nobody appeared eager to offer up information. He looked at Yuki and immediately knew that she hadn't been visited yet. Her parents were too loud for Nanette's sensibilities. Plus, Yuki was just a toddler—how could anyone so young be a target for a grown woman's misguided quest? No, Nanette had more commonsense for that. Joey calculated that she could have hit Meadow's home. It was gigantic. He imagined it would be easy for an intruder to go unnoticed as long as she got over the fence okay. But the more Joey thought about the kids, the less able he was to believe any of them were spied on by Nanette. Javier's grandmother was always home. There was no way she wouldn't have seen her. The Allaways lived in an intimate apartment complex—Nanette wouldn't even be able to get into the building.

Joey set his fork down. It clinked against the plate, gaining the attention of the kids closest to him. His chair squeaked against the floor as he stood up and said, "Rich, can we talk in the garden really quickly?"

Stammering, Rich agreed as all of the kids went *ooooooooohhh*.

After Rich, Figgy was the first to her feet. Rich and Joey went into the upstairs bathroom and shut the door. The Badgers knew that they were supposed to keep on doing whatever it was that they were doing when this happened. Except for maybe Javier, who needed to be held back by Meadow grabbing the collar of his shirt. Meadow ushered Figgy to go follow Mister Joey and Mister Rich but Figgy wouldn't budge any farther than the kitchen door.

She shouldn't have had to be the one to go anyway. She wasn't the last one to play Miss Nanette. That was Yuki, but since Yuki would be too afraid to go spy on the grownups, the responsibility would have to fall to the next in the Nanette lineage: Meadow Descoteaux.

Meadow was a tactful and spry young spy who was having none of Figgy's shenanigans. Except for Jon and Roux, who were pleasantly passing their lunch together with Jon occasionally making an unimportant joke or sweet comment, the kids congregated at the closed door to the hallway. Nearest to the door stood Figgy and Meadow. Javier was off to the side. Swarming the seven-year-old girls were all the younger Badgers. In the back of the mob was the unspeaking Tenth Child, who was almost separate from the throng altogether. But meshed together were the twins and the little ones urging somebody to go play Miss Nanette on Mister Joey and Mister Rich.

"I'm not going out there," Meadow said, knowing that whoever played Miss Nanette always lost.

"We'll be right here behind you," Figgy assured. If things went awry, Figgy was the only one of the kids who wouldn't bail on Meadow. "And it's your turn."

"It's the baby's turn."

Whispering into Meadow's ear, Figgy said, "Do you trust her with this mission?"

Meadow sighed and entered the hallway.

Meadow walked up the hall, turned around, and saw seven heads poking through kitchen doorway. She tiptoed along the carpet to better hear the mumblings beyond the bathroom door.

"I can't believe you want to do this," she heard Mister Rich say.

"I don't want to but I feel like I should help," Mister Joey replied.

At the sound of footsteps, Meadow retreated. She barreled into the crowd of other kids in the doorway to the kitchen, toppling over onto Figgy. They fell onto the tiles.

"You're Miss Nanette next," Meadow said.

"It's not my turn," Figgy protested.

"Then someone else is Miss Nanette—I'm not snooping anymore."

"What's this now?" Joey asked as he and Rich entered the kitchen. "What about Miss Nanette?"

"Meadow, come off of Figgy," Rich told as he picked her up.

"I didn't do anything!"

"Then you wouldn't mind getting off Figgy."

Meadow grumbled as she got to her feet. Javier helped up Figgy who was unfazed by the accidental scuffle. Rich brought all the kids back to lunch. He had thought that the kids just played a little spoof on them.

Joey was not so easily fooled.

They were playing a game, Joey thought as he lay across the couch after the Fieldings were just taken home. They were playing a game about Nanette and sneaking around. Had this been the first time he saw them do that? Maybe, but he didn't like the idea of where the kids would have thought of such a playtime scandal. From what he could tell from his copious amounts of time around the youthfully inclined, Joey knew that kids often were an unfiltered compilation of everything around them. Nanette wasn't likely to open up to these kids about her missing lunchbox, so what were the odds that something had gone wonky in the field?

Hypothetically, Nanette goes into a house and hides from the parents. It wasn't unlikely for a child to be sneaking around after bedtime at the same moment as Nanette. Say that she had run into a kid and that kid (rather than tell their parents) comes back to daycare and then turns it into a game whereby the grownups get snooped on. Could Nanette have been less than truthful with her tactful stealth?

He spoke about these romps briefly with Rich. And he wanted in. At least, he wanted in for one big hurrah. If it was so important to the house then why should he be kept out of the equation? Plus, she had come so far with the children's houses with so few results—if this was going to end then it needed to end fast. The three had exchanged select, calculated words since the bedroom debacle the night before and he didn't know, or see, any other way to smooth the relations out.

Rich paced the bedroom floor. He couldn't sit. He couldn't nap. He could only listen to the occasional steps of Joey up above. Work was over for the day, so that wasn't even available to preoccupy him. Had he overplayed his hand last night?

He took to cleaning the clothes off of the floor.

Last night, he came to terms with his deeds. Weed in the closet was its own thing. He had made peace with that, but not with the discomfort that followed Nanette knowing about its presence. Not to mention that he couldn't even garden to calm himself because he and Joey already agreed to move on from that part of their careers.

Was it called? Aiding and abetting? Were those his crimes tied to Nanette's stupid lunchbox? He used to be an average man. Not particularly good, but not bad. After all, he had gotten invited into those homes. Hell, one of them was just him asking if the lunchbox was there—and the woman helped him search.

Au contraire, he thought. Something else was in play.

The crimes were in the past (hopefully) but the lunchbox was still missing. He could only imagine why Nanette was handling it so well.

Nanette was about to explode. She walked circles around

her office until her trail wore away at the carpet. Pinned up on the wall was a printed version of her spreadsheet.

In bleeding red ink she had marked off six children. Six unsuccessful leads. Two boys, four girls, all were guilty until forlornly proven innocent. If she was asked, Nanette would still admit that she thought any of the children could still be the thief. It was just less likely that these ones marked off on the chart were the culprit.

Her phone rang. She saw it was Grandmother and ignored the call.

She held her hands behind her back. Though Nanette was blind to the sensation, her left eye was twitching. Her vision was like a poor television connection. But she had tuned it out to focus on the task at hand.

She was running out of children.

Though she was positive one of them had it… it was probable that she would have found it by now. Six children done. Sixty percent of the way through. And still, Nanette with a well running dry. She looked at her options: boy who doesn't shut up, red-headed girl, loud girl, and the last one. Nanette's first thought was that the red-headed girl, the quiet one, she was the thief. The coy little klepto with her silence to hide behind. Or maybe that was too obvious. Or maybe not—she couldn't start second-guessing herself.

If Nanette Abbot could trust one thing in this world, it was Nanette Abbot.

There was a knock on her office door. Rather than letting anyone inside (seeing how it was her home office and she preferred to retain what few secrets remained in the home) she met the caller in the hall.

"Joseph?" she said. Rich was standing behind him, looking elsewhere.

"You're not going to like this," Joey plainly said, "but I want in."

What Meadow Descoteaux didn't know was that her house was much larger than the needs of three people. There were six bedrooms, two of which were lived in. The others were places for Mister Descoteaux's business associates. Mister Descoteaux himself kept the master bedroom that had its own en suite, opened up onto a private patio, and held several antiquities and luxuries that he thought necessary for happy living. These high scale accoutrements included things like a mounted rhinoceros head (it was fake but Mister Descoteaux did not know that), an ivory baby grand piano (not real ivory, this Mister Descoteaux did know), and a coat of arms that he designed himself and had embroidered onto a tapestry hanging between two long standing mirrors.

As was to be expected with Mister Descoteaux, his indisputable taste for the quote-unquote finer things was rooted in a misunderstood insecurity that his father made him repress at a young age. Mister Descoteaux would never admit to wanting to be loved the way his father loved that hot rod he had restored in the summertimes in that dusty garage south of Boston. Mostly, he would never admit it because he claimed to have no love for his father other than a grand respect for his business sense.

Perhaps if Mister Descoteaux had a good cry then he'd be able to understand why his father's apathy bothers him so, or maybe it would help him understand why his wife, Chunhua, disappeared after ten years of marriage. But no, Mister Descoteaux was just an average dude—he liked things, and getting on. And, yes, he loved his daughter.

He'd found a nanny for Meadow to shuttle her back and forth from school and Baby Badger Cub Club. Descoteaux liked the guys there. He'd known Rich from working with his father. The Eliot Paper Factory (now Eliot Paper Company) was the main supplier of stationary and other ephemera to Descoteaux Limited. It was a shame that the Eliots turned on Richie like that, so young, so hardened to the world. Mister Descoteaux was willing to do anything to help that boy. Except maybe offer him a place to stay or a hot meal. No, "anything" in this context really just meant that he'd buy weed off of them and then let them socialize his daughter.

The capacious halls of the Descoteaux home served no

purpose than to help Mister Descoteaux feel successful. He was of the mindset that whoever died with the most toys won. Which was why he owned four unused ATVs, two boats, and a stagecoach that he'd won at a charity auction. None of these things did he play with when he had free time. Once or twice a week he would be out with his buddies from work or college and they'd drink or try to meet women.

Since Chunhua left, it had to be said, Mister Descoteaux had trouble spending time with his daughter because there was no one to yell at him to do so. And ignoring her was easier to do than to accept that he was just a bad father. He thought that he was okay, but he expected that his wife would just be a better father to their daughter than his own father was to him. It was all rather simple when one took the time to boil it down: father didn't show him affection so he became successful at business so he met his wife so he could have a daughter so she could have a better life but the wife disappears and the husband becomes just like his father so the only logical step is to buy a stagecoach at a charity auction.

Such was the ballad of Roger Descoteaux.

In his pursuits to fill his life with things, he invested in the mansion which his associates called an "estate" but the word was a bit too hoity-toity for his tastes. So it was just a large house. Surrounding the grounds was a wrought iron fence with an automatic gate. Chunhua used to urge him to invest in a security system but Mister Descoteaux never saw it necessary when he had such a nice fence. Plus, if a burglar ever did make it inside then he could just introduce them to his set of old hunting rifles. They'd either fear him or join him.

Far behind the house, balancing himself atop the iron fence, sat Joey Abbot reaching down to hoist up Nanette. Rich was giving her a lift from below and she was struggling to accept their assistance. Joey would offer her his hand and she would slap it away before realizing she needed it to get up. Joey had been the only one athletic enough to scale the fence on his own.

When they got Nanette to the top, she instantly hopped

down into the yard. As much as Richard leapt, he couldn't get high enough, or a sure enough footing, to surmount the fence. Nanette only got up because Joey pulled from the top with Rich pushing from the bottom, with no one to give Rich a lift, he reached the others. As Nanette began to walk towards the mansion, Rich asked, "Are you just going to leave me here?"

"If you cannot overcome the fence, then you cannot overcome the fence," Nanette shrugged.

"But I helped you."

"And for that I will likely be grateful."

Joey, who was still on the fence, didn't know which person he should go with.

"It should be said," Nanette said, "that I only needed the address, not assistance."

"Go with her," Rich told Joey, almost out of spite. He begrudged, "I'll keep the car running."

Joey dropped to the ground beside Nanette. He heard her phone go off, but she silenced it quick. Rich held on to the iron bars of the fence as Joey faced him.

"Be great in there," Rich advised.

"I will."

"Oh, goodness. A lovely time for a heartfelt farewell," Nanette griped. "I will commence the operation with or without you, Joseph."

The cousins set off for the house. Walking by so many different courts that were underutilized, they took stock of the backyard: pool, Jacuzzi, bocce court, horseshoe pins, tennis court, volleyball net (with gear for badminton off to the side), shuffleboard, croquet, squash, lawn darts, ladder golf, disc golf, three holes for mini golf, a fire pit, a second pool, an island with a built-in propane grill, and a collection of porcelain garden gnomes.

They approached a glass door at the back of the house. Nanette pushed Joey aside as she reached for the handle. When it wouldn't turn, Nanette narrowed her eyes at it and tried once more to open it. The locked state of the door perplexed her. Meanwhile, Joey was considering their alternative options. He saw nearby there was a little rock garden. Skeptical of what he could find there, he sifted through the various stones. He thought to himself, There's no way anybody has one of these anymore. But just as he doubted, he found a rock in the garden about the size of a tennis ball. It felt like plastic in his hands so he brought it back to Nanette.

Nanette looked at the rock and took it. She then tossed it to the ground, thinking that Joey was stupid for offering to break the glass of the door. Joey, ignoring her, picked it back up and rattled it next to his ear. There was a soft thudding noise inside the rock. He popped it open and found a small, rusty key. Trying it in the doorway, Joey got them inside within the minute.

Rich stood alone, kicking at some dirt, uselessly. He eyed the house, positive that he had been stranded by his … partners in crime seemed too drastic a phrase. Thinking about the ordeal of the past couple days, he kicked the dirt off his shoe and went back to the car.

Twenty minutes later, Rich found himself standing inside the doorway to a Kay Jewelers when a frightfully frog-looking man, with dimensions not completely unlike a marble, asked him, "May I help you?"

"Yes," Rich replied, "I'm looking for a ring."

Joey and Nanette first noticed the superfluous amount of everything. After ten minutes spent roaming the halls of the Descoteaux mansion, the thin film of dust over everything and the untended nature of all the aging appliances, gave them the impression that nobody used this part of the house. Nanette thought that it was dangerous to not use one's entire home because one never knows when there's a covert opium operation in the basement.

After a few more minutes of traipsing the corridors, at a regular volume Joey said, "Do we know where we're going?"

"No we do not, Misses de Winter," Nanette replied. "Who would have been able to guess that we would require a map for this labyrinth?"

"I think I see some stairs."

They carried on. They found unsettling amounts of plates and bowls, all in fine wooden cabinets. Look at all that teak, Nanette thought while looking at the mahogany furniture. Tapestries of mountains and stylistic paintings of rivers covered the walls. It was a depressing museum. All the beautiful pieces went unloved and unadmired in this unused quarter of the building.

Joey stepped into a gallery of sorts in his pursuit of the staircase when Nanette grabbed his elbow.

"Let me go," Joey said.

"Do you hear that?"

"It's your phone."

He wasn't wrong. Nanette ignored another call from Grandmother. "Not that," she said. Softly, far off, she heard the tittering of movement across tile.

"I don't hear anything."

"Wait here."

"Yeah, okay."

Nanette veered off, winding her way around an assortment of bookcases and freestanding hutches. She didn't have a gun, but she did put her fingers into the shape of a gun in hopes of scaring someone if they only happened to see her silhouette.

Eventually, Nanette arrived at a curtain hanging up between two bookcases stacked with cups and canned foods. Unlike the plates in the other cabinets, these cups had residue around their rims and stank of food. She pulled back the curtain to reveal a little room built behind the bookcases. There was a cot dressed with a rug instead of a sheet next to a pile of antique books. A wash basin was opposite from the cot. For light, a dim chandelier hung down into the makeshift room. Lost in momentary awe, the room distracted Nanette as the curtain was pulled back by someone else.

"Who are you?!" barked a woman Nanette had never seen before. Nanette leapt.

"Joseph!" Nanette called out.

"Who's Joseph?" the woman asked. "Where did you come from?"

Joey called back, "What is it?"

"There's a Chinese woman down here."

The woman huffed.

"Is it important that she's Chinese?" Joey called. "Why is that her defining feature?"

"Do you want to have this discussion now, Joseph? Is it really important?"

"It's important to her."

"Who are you?" the woman barked.

"We will get to that," Nanette said. "More importantly, who are you?"

"Where did you come from?"

"Outside."

"What?! But the door… it's been locked. I've learned not to travel that far for fear of losing hope."

"What? Who are you, woman?"

"My name is Chunhua Descoteaux. I've been lost down here for three years."

"Well that's disconcerting," Joey said as he and Nanette sat on Chunhua's cot. She brought them some tea that she had scavenged some months back. Chunhua had just relayed to the cousins about the time she had spent down there. Foraging among the antiques that she and her husband had collected over the years. She loved her husband but he was an idiot.

Chunhua had made the mistake one day of passing through the garage when her husband went out to a charity auction. There was a storage house tacked onto the mansion and the only way to caravan was through the garage. She wanted to find some old vase for their fourth guest bedroom because she was going for a "look." When she attempted to return back into the mansion proper, Chunhua was trapped because the door would not budge. Peering through the keyhole, she was able to see an old stagecoach blocking her passage. She couldn't blame Roger for the purchase though: after all, she, too, liked the acquisition of things.

"I made it to the far door to the back yard, but it was locked and the glass was made to withstand hurricanes."

"Hurricanes? In Massachusetts?"

"That's not the point. The point was that it was strong glass."

"That's all well and good," Nanette said, rising, "but it is obvious what we came for is not in this location. Where in your home is the kitchen?"

"Netty," Joey interjected. "Chunhua, we can bring you home. We unlocked that door."

"Then I shall show you to the kitchen," Chunhua smiled. "Tell me, Netty, what is it that you have lost?"

The doorbell sang. Joey, Nanette, and Chunhua stood behind the roman columns at the front of the house waiting for someone to retrieve them. It had been the first time in three years Chunhua stood in direct sunlight. She kept positioning herself in the shade. Joey imagined there was music playing.

Finally, Roger Descoteaux appeared in the doorway.

"Chunhua?" he said, immediately stifling his urge to cry.

"It's me, Roger. I have missed you so."

He rushed over and took her in his arms "I thought you'd left forever!"

"Never! Never! Things just got complicated, but these wonderful people found me."

"Is there anything we can do for them?"

"Well…" Nanette stepped forward.

Minutes later, Nanette was silencing her phone again in the kitchen while Joey prowled through the drawers. Chunhua and Roger sat nearby, ignorant to the Abbots tearing through their kitchen. Joey was surprised when Roger didn't recognize him, but then again Rich was the one who had known him beforehand and the nanny was the one who catered to Meadow's needs.

Shortly after, Chunhua left the kitchen. Roger sat there holding in the tears his father had shamed him for having. Chunhua returned with a sleepy Meadow in her arms

"Mom?" Meadow squeaked, not fully understanding the situation.

"I know, Meadow, it's me. But I want you to say hello to some special people. This is Mister Joey and Miss Nanette."

"Huh?" said the girl.

"Hi, Meadow," Joey chirped.

"Mister Joey!" Meadow said, pushing away from her mother. She ran over to Joey and hugged his legs. She then looked over to Nanette and frowned.

She was supposed to help Nanette hide! But here she was in view of both of her parents! The game was rigged against her!

Sensing some displeasure, Joey asked, "What's up, Meadow?"

And she replied, "You can't win the game. You can try but you can't win the game."

"Preposterous," Nanette said at full volume though she thought it was *sotto voce.*

Ominous, Joey thought.

Chunhua picked her daughter back up and carried her off to her bedroom. She wanted to see how much Meadow had grown since preschool and wondered if she even remembered her. Roger was relieved because he could worry less about recognizing how bad of a father he was.

Then Nanette's phone went off again. Her official reason for not silencing it was in the case of a work related call she needed to be ready, the unofficial reason was that she didn't know how. The incessant peal gave Nanette heart palpitations, like the Porter answering the knocks on the door.

"That's, what, the eleventh phone call today?" Joey asked.

"You should answer it."

"It's unimportant, surely," Nanette said.

"You know," Roger Descoteaux said, getting up from his seat and refilling his glass, "you shouldn't let a phone call go unanswered because of spite. It's not healthy to keep this bottled up."

On the word "up" Mister Descoteaux accidentally yet passionately crushed his glass in his hand.

"Oh would you look at that," he said, "I'm bleeding."

And he left the room to treat it.

Joey stepped away from the drawers, declaring that the lunchbox—safe to say—was not in the Descoteaux residence. He listened to the outdated melody of Nanette's ringtone play yet again.

"Answer it," Joey said.

"No."

"Why not?"

"Because I know what she has to say."

"And what's that?"

Nanette paused. "That is unimportant."

"Then it should be easy to answer it."

"No."

Joey snuck up behind Nanette and stole her phone out of her pocket. "I'll talk to her. She's my grandmother, too."

"No! She has nothing to say to you!"

This was it. She was going to lose him. Nanette felt the gravity pulling Joseph away from her.

"Why not?"

"Because she does not. It is just the way it is."

Grandmother will tell him. She will ruin them just like she always could. She'll take the final dregs of Nanette's power away.

"Come on, Netty, why can't I know?"

"You can know."

"I can?"

"But it is not important. We are getting dizzy going around in so many circles, are we not?"

This is the end.

"Okay…" Joey stepped back. He held up the still ringing phone. "What aren't you telling me?"

"Fine! Answer the darn phone!"

He did.

"Gran?" he said.

"Joseph? Didn't expect you to answer Nanette's phone." Her voice sounded sweet like it usually did.

Joey watched Nanette look at him on the phone. She was almost doubling over, like cement was solidifying in her stomach. She clutched the countertop for support.

Nanette couldn't let Grandmother play her this way. She wouldn't allow it.

"Yeah, she doesn't want me to talk to you for some reason."

"Oh, how odd. I was just calling because I think I found her lunchbox—"

But Joey didn't hear the end of the sentence.

Nanette had charged him to grab her phone.

She got it back, instinctually whipping it against the wall.

The screen shattered into a spider web pattern and the back casing splintered off.

Nanette sunk to her knees.

"Nanette, what the hell?" Joey asked.

"She cannot tell you!" Nanette almost wept. "She cannot tell you!"

"Tell me what, Nanette? What the hell is wrong?"

"She can't tell you that I told them."

"What? What? Told who what?"

"Your parents."

"What about them?"

"I told them, Joey. I told them you were gay."

CHAPTER TWELVE

THE HAND PUPPET FIASCO OF 2006

Ten years ago, there was a fresh, sealed pack of brown paper bags sitting on a table. Norma Abbot had placed out arts and crafts supplies for all the kids. The table was covered with jars of glitter, pipe cleaners, googly eyes, scented markers, and acrylic paints. It was clear that Norma had been getting on in years and distant from the family because the youngest, Joseph, was fourteen years old and bragging about his girlfriend. Nanette, who by then was twenty-two, wouldn't even honor the notion of participating in such frivolity.

But Joey was less resistant. He sat with his cousins Eeny, Meeny, Miny, Mo, and Larry as they groaned—urged by their parents to humor their grandmother. They didn't need to argue much seeing how the kids all liked Grandmother and, regardless of her dated activities, wanted to see her happy.

The goal was to get the kids to make some hand puppets—a fun activity that came to Grandmother from the art classes at which she had volunteered to help look after children. But the kids just sat around, uneventfully. One of them was just tapping a plastic bottle of paint against the table. Another was rearranging the googly eyes by size. And another was just face down in a pile of felt, snoring.

Inside, the parents were drinking. It was the old Abbot summer home and the family thought it would be good for them to all spend a vacation together at least once a year since the kids were getting older. The vacation home had many beds and enough bathrooms to keep everybody from breathing on everybody else but somehow family finds a way. In the corner, in his favorite recliner, with a Heineken in one hand and a dead television remote in the other, sat Grandpa Horatio Abbot. He was the kind of guy who coughed after every word he said. Horatio was also a husk of a person—Horatio didn't like to eat food anymore because everything tasted bland. In the past, a cheeseburger, a real American cheeseburger, used to be so greasy and packed with flavor that he would have to spend a day in the hospital. Nowadays, people let vegetarians into their homes and that was enough to transform Horatio into a grouchy codger. That year they were also celebrating his birthday even if he didn't want to. He wouldn't be able to blow out the candles on his own birthday cake now without losing consciousness.

Grandmother was leading a crew of her children to help her cook in the kitchen. She was making pizzas. It was a good group food, and popular with people of every age. Norma Abbot took pride in coordination.

She slid her pizzas into the oven and wondered how the arts and crafts project was going.

It wasn't. The quintuplets were entirely unsuccessful in even getting the brown paper bags out of the plastic encasing. One by one, the cousins became content with the idea of not playing around with this baby project. It was only Joey who picked up the pack of paper bags and tried more than once to tear it open.

He pulled and tugged and tried using his teeth until the plastic was warped and misshapen. Joey worked until one could see the individual veins in his arm. Nanette, who believed herself the smartest out of the entire family (not just her impudent cousins), had decided to take pity on the others. She got up and approached the arts and crafts table. As if her undergrad degree was a signifier of her ability to tear open plastic covers, she snatched the block out of Joey's hands and scoffed to make sure he knew that there was some condescending going on.

Confident in her abilities to make something happen, Nanette too failed to make anything happen.

She twisted and bit, she mangled and scratched, she bumped, thumped, plopped, dropped, bopped, tossed, flipped, flopped, socked, rocked, grunted, punted, punched, bunched, squeezed, squashed, stomped, stamped, tamped, and berated. But nothing continued to happen rather devoutly.

"Let me help you, Nanette," Joey advised.

"But look at all the control that I have this situation under, Joseph," Nanette said, turning her back to him.

But he kept offering, and she kept denying. Until he stopped offering and began insisting that it was his turn again to try. Nanette wouldn't let him close to the pack for fear that all the effort she had already put in would have been for nothing. Not to mention that she would appear foolish if she couldn't get the bag open after demonstrating how superior she was.

Neither of them particularly wanted to make hand puppets, but this wasn't about that anymore. Either pride or desire had consumed their motivation for the present task. In the middle of Nanette's yanking at the plastic, Joey made a leap to snatch the pack.

He got his hands on it, but the move wasn't thorough enough for him to unarm Nanette. The two cousins each had a hand on the indestructible packaging. Nanette pulled in such a manner to try and loosen Joey's grip. Joey was not nearly as thoughtful and was just tearing at the package in the honest effort to start an arts and craft project of which he thought himself too old to do. The other cousins had surrounded Joey and Nanette and cheered them on thinking that they were about to start a fight. Nanette tried to shake Joey, but with every jerk and jarring motion he just pulled himself closer to the pack.

And back inside the kitchen, Grandmother was pulling the pizzas out of the oven when Joey and Nanette burst through the door. While all the parents scrambled to separate the twosome, Grandmother left to tell her husband that dinner would be ready soon.

The parents were too slow, and Joey and Nanette were too slippery. They crusaded through the kitchen with little regard to chairs and the tinier members of the family. They charged through the home until ending up right beside their grandfather, Horatio. Grandmother had just whispered something in his ear about dinner and, upon seeing Joey and Nanette, was horribly startled with the proceedings.

The elder's wide-eyed expression went unnoticed as the proud duo, with an ultimate heave, ripped apart the plastic casing and launched brown paper bags everywhere. Grandmother jumped away from Horatio's side as the bags came raining down on him.

The house was silent for a moment after the final bag hit the ground.

Grandmother stepped back toward Horatio in his chair. He wasn't moving. She slowly reached to check his pulse and said, "Oh dear, your grandfather's heart just gave out!"

"Yes," Nanette said, between weighted breaths, "but the bag is open."

The note on the refrigerator door said that Baby Badger Cub Club would be closed for the rest of the week. The note hinted at indefiniteness, but Nanette was not able to read that much into it.

What she figured was that Joey and Rich would be back by the end of the week. They wouldn't be able to last that long without her remarkable assistance and resources. Perhaps more importantly, Nanette needed them to bring the kids here because there were still three children who needed the inquisition. She was so close to finding her lunchbox. She imagined the glory of having the ham and cheese returned to her, to avenge the fallen ham and cheese day. But she couldn't do that without those darn children and their sticky little hands coming into the light of justice.

The thought terrified Nanette—for a fraction of an instant, she worried that she might not find her lunchbox. There was the fear that her lunchbox might be lost to the annals of history, encrusted with the unsavory flavor of unresolved mysteries. Then she buried the notion underneath all the other things she'd rather not think about.

Instead she speculated how many more minutes Joseph and Richard would need until they walked through the front door. Though she didn't care where they were—those mooches may finally be doing a chore like picking up something for the benefit of the house or something—they weren't worth so much of Nanette's concern. If she was lucky, maybe they were printing out a list of addresses for her to investigate so they went to get the list laminated because they knew how much Nanette admires quality lamination.

She paced the floor of her home office.

Nanette had tried sitting still but the silence of the home unseated her.

Usually the bustle of a boy in the kitchen would echo in the background. Or she would hear one of Rich's weird show tunes playing on the radio. Or it could even be one of Joey's personality-less crime dramas for which he had some critical affinity. Perhaps the most striking was the lack of a childish shriek. There was no exhausting youth parading about her home like a giddy vagrant, a doped-up sugar fiend. And because the daycare was closed today, there wasn't even the ethereal suggestion of life. Nanette didn't remember solitude this way. The house hadn't been this empty for years.

She took to pacing between her office and the kitchen, the entire length of the upstairs hall.

It couldn't have been anything she had said or done, Nanette speculated. It was likely that the boys weren't home because they got mixed up with a drug cartel and were shipped to Columbia or Mexico or, she didn't know, Delaware, and needed her to get them out of trouble. Or it could be that they were swingers and just mixed up with the wrong couple. Now to fight for freedom they had to rely on their charms to protect them. Oh no, Nanette worried—those boys were the least charming people she knew. It also occurred to Nanette that she might not know exactly what a swinger is.

She thought back to yesterday.

After telling Joey that she uncloseted him to his own parents, he had seemed—one may argue—upset. He rode back to the house without speaking. Even to Rich, he said nothing. It wasn't until they all got home and Joey shut up in his room that Nanette could hear any mumblings from him. They all went to bed as usual. And the next day, Nanette went to work as usual.

The unusual was Nanette's inability to search the next house for her lunchbox.

What was wrong with Joseph anyhow?

It seemed that he was rather hung up on this little fact that Nanette had happened to divulge unto his family. It was not as if it was untrue. Joseph Abbot was a man who loved a man. How was she to know that his own parents would not have been as accepting? Nanette, frankly, had more important things to worry about than other people's homosexuality. And then, rather than having to lie to himself or to his parents, Nanette had done him this kindness and effectively hid it from him for two years.

Nanette began pacing up and down the staircase.

The sound of her footsteps soothed.

She found herself at Joey and Rich's bedroom door. It was pulled tight, and there wasn't the burning aroma of a scented candle wafting through the walls. They were probably just napping, shirking the day away. To test this hypothesis, Nanette let herself into the bedroom.

But it was just her in there. The room was tidy. The bedding was made smoothly. The chair was pushed into the desk. All the clothes on the racks were arranged in an orderly fashion; there was no wayward sleeve in the room. Nanette opened up the closet door to find two decommissioned tents with beds of soil at the bottom. The closet was dark and nothing was growing there.

She sat down at the desk and ran her hand across the flat surface. It was cool to her touch. Nanette picked a pen out of a cup and began to click the button against the desk. Examining the desk further, she saw a drawer for files built into it.

The drawer opened with a clunk. In there she found a collection of manila folders all with tabs that read familiar names. *Allaway, Figgy; Bolivar, Javier; Descoteaux, Meadow; Dodd, Virginia; Dodd, Zola.* And she stopped thumbing when she arrived at a folder labeled: *Fielding, Paxton.*

She pulled the file and laid it out on the desk. Glossing over the boring facts about emergency contacts, allergies, medications, she found what she needed.

Nanette cleaned up the file and returned it.

Then she made a dash for her keys.

CHAPTER THIRTEEN

ROUX AND PAX FIELDING

This might have been the coolest day of Roux's life. But it was definitely the coolest day of Pax's life because he had fewer to compare it too.

They helped their father pull out the bed from the guest room couch and dress it with some fresh sheets. Usually, only guests like some of their parents' old friends or Grandma Fielding would stay in the guestroom, but not anymore. While their mother poured drinks in the kitchen, Pax dragged one of the suitcases into the guestroom and Roux carried the other two. Everything needed to be perfect because they didn't know if Mister Joey and Mister Rich would ever be staying with them again.

The house itself was nestled in a wooded hamlet. It was taller than it was wide. The Fieldings were particularly fond of the latticework covering the sides of the home and had ivy vines running up them. There was no garage or central ventilation, but it was a simple sort of living that attracted the Fieldings in the first place.

They had arrived not too long ago. Mister and Doctor Fielding had let the kids know about the abrupt company when they went to pick them up from the sitter. It was a shame with

171

Baby Badger closed for a couple days, leaving the parents scrambling to find someone to watch their kids, or a program that would take them last minute. Tomorrow would be a different story though, because they could just leave the kids at home with the boys and it wouldn't be much different from any normal day.

As for the guys, Callie and Al were glad to take them in. When Joey called needing a place to stay for a while, they'd said yes first and figured they could ask questions later. The Fieldings had never seen a sad or particularly angry side of Joey before, so when he called sounding somewhat shaken, they had insisted on opening up their house to them. It wasn't like they didn't have the space. And, of course, the arrangement would be different if the kids hated the boys. But fortunately things had come together in this procession of misfortunes.

So, the grownups drank and chatted in the kitchen with the kids at their heels. When Pax finished up his portion of help, he kept asking Mister Rich questions.

"Are you guys sharing a bed?"

"Yes, Pax."

"Do you always share a bed?"

"Usually."

"Do you have a bunk bed?"

"No, Pax."

"I want a bunk bed."

"Why's that?"

"Because you can sleep twice as hard in a bunk bed. Do, do, do you like sleeping?"

"Yes."

"Do you dream?"

"I do sometimes. Do you?"

"What do you dream about?"

"Oh, I don't know. Singing, I guess. Forests, sometimes."

"Do you ever, you ever, um, sing in a forest in a dream?"

"I don't know, Pax. Doesn't that sound a little crazy?"

"It's not crazy!"

"Then yes, all the time."

It wasn't long until Pax's voice tired itself out. The toddler didn't think to ask questions about why Joey and Rich were there or how long they had planned on staying. Everything, at least for today, was tilted towards discussion of bunk beds which, though he did not have one, was the chief preoccupation of Pax Fielding's thoughts.

After a while, Al Fielding picked up Pax and took him off to bed. His bedtime was much earlier than his sister's, but Roux didn't need one, seeing as how she went to bed on her own accord at a fairly consistent time. Presently, Roux left Misters Joey and Rich alone so she could read a book Jon had recommended to her in the den. Focusing was difficult due to her excitement with the houseguests, so after resigning herself to sitting with the book on her lap, Roux let herself be comforted by the sounds of conversation coming through the walls.

When the grownups were essentially by themselves, with little but alcohol and friendly chatter to pass the time, Joey and Rich revealed as much as they thought was necessary. They told the Fieldings about how Nanette had gotten to be a bit much but withheld the specifics of her actions. They told them that she hadn't been the same since the vanishing of her idiotic lunchbox, but hid the actions she took to try and get it back.

In fact, even part of why they ended up at the Fieldings' was not clear to Rich. He just knew that something had hurt Joey inside of the Descoteaux mansion. Rich didn't need specifics of how that … operation went, but he would like to know why Joey had to escape.

"Well," Al said after finishing his drink, "it's not like Nanette will do anything too dramatic, you know. It's just a lunchbox."

Rich forced out a chuckle.

"Yeah maybe," said Joey. "Thanks again for all of this. We just need a couple days until we figure out what comes next."

"Are you going back home after Nanette cools down?"

"I don't know if it is Nanette who needs to cool down."

"Nanette's probably," Rich jumped in, "as cool as she will be for some time."

"You guys should settle in," Callie said. "The bed's not amazing but it's still a decent night's rest. Unpack and we'll have a drink later."

"Sounds like a plan. We'll unpack, thank you."

Al took the guys' empties and put them in the recycling. Rich took Joey by the arm, following Callie to their room. The kids had stacked the suitcases on top of one another by the closet which only had a vacuum and some cleaning supplies in it. She then switched on and off the light switch and told them that the window had a hard time opening but it could get there with enough hard love. Then they were left alone.

Rich perched on the corner of the mattress. He sunk through it enough to feel uncomfortable sitting there. He pushed himself further onto the bed, running his hands over the embroidery of the comforter. Joey kept standing, examining the room. There was a dresser that he investigated with a vanity mirror, the drawers were all mostly empty except for some spare sheets. A potted ficus sat in the corner but Joey was pretty sure it was just plastic.

"You want to tell me what exactly's going on?" Rich asked while adjusting a pillow.

"Yeah, I do," he said.

Nanette parked in an alcove off the side of the drive. The many trees would make it easy for her to sneak up to the house. Though the sun was setting, and the orange sky was turning to purple as she walked, the air was still warm and filled with determination.

She noted as she approached the house that only a few of the windows were illuminated.

The glint from the interior contoured the ivy leaves. This gave Nanette an idea from almost every television show she saw when she was little.

She came up to the lattice which stretched the height of

the home. It was a series of interconnected brown diamonds that provided a foothold for countless petals. Nanette gripped the lattice, uncomfortable with the splintery feel of the wood in her hands. It made her wonder that the lattice might not have been made of teak, but she knew in the end that it had to be. She was an expert in identifying teak. Taking her first steps, Nanette placed her feet in two of the lowest diamonds and, as she pulled herself up, the wood crumbled under her weight.

The lattice disintegrated beneath her shoes and instantly she was standing on the ground again. She tried again on another part of wall, but still the wood broke under her. On the third attempt, she couldn't even get a handhold because the wood broke off in her grip. Perhaps, Nanette pontificated, the things that happen on television do not happen in real life for a reason. After all, climbing the side of a house was a ludicrous pipedream. This was the real world where real things happened, like finding a long-lost wife in some millionaire's basement or there being a child of whom no one knows the name or face.

Instead, Nanette found a dark window that reflected her image. She wouldn't meet her eyes. Rather, she investigated the sill in an effort to open the aperture from the outside. Using her palms instead of her fingers, she pushed against the middle of the window to see if she could get the pane up. The window retaliated with some resistance. She readjusted and tried again.

The window thumped open.

Nanette heaved herself in. She landed on her palms, feeling worn carpet under her. Moving her hands across the floor, Nanette felt a chilly, plastic tub pushed up against a wall. She followed the wall until she could tell when the molding went vertical. Nanette had found the door and used the knob to pull herself up. She groped the wall in order to find a light switch.

She flipped the lights on and promptly came face-to-face with Pax Fielding standing up in his crib looking at her.

Nanette was a moment away from complaining about the situation when Pax hurriedly pointed across the room. He was pointing at a gray baby monitor on top of the dresser. Hugging the wall, Nanette sidled up to it, shutting it off.

"Now they can't find you," Pax said.

"No they cannot," she said as if it was gratitude. Nanette made a break for the exit.

"Wait!" Pax said. "You aren't going without me! I'm ready!"

"For what?"

"I'm helping you spy! Like the other kids."

"I need no help, child."

"I have to come with you."

"Or else what?"

"I'll tell on you."

"Wow, I am truly shaking. You are an embryo in a cage. How helpful can you be to me?"

"I know the house."

"Do you know where the kitchen is?"

"Yes!"

Nanette scrunched up her face. She watched the prisoner behind his crib bars, bouncing with anticipation. She sniffled. It was likely that he knew the layout of the house which could prove effective in shortening the operation.

"Alright, inmate," Nanette said, lifting Pax out of the crib and setting him on the floor, "but a few rules: you carry your own weight, you don't ask questions, and you follow orders."

"What are orders?" he asked.

"You are already in violation of the rules."

"You're in volition of the rules."

"That does not even make sense. Do you hear yourself?"

"You don't hear yourself."

"You cannot play me for a fool, child. Show me the kitchen and keep your head down."

"Wait!"

"You do not give orders!"

Pax waddled over to his crib and pulled a pale blue blanket through the space in between the bars. He handed the tiny rectangle of fabric to Nanette.

"To hide," Pax said.

"How long must I carry this?" Nanette groaned as she took the blanket from him.

"It'll help you."

"Fine," Nanette shoved it into her back pocket. "But be quiet."

Pax nodded. And then added, "I will."

He then gestured to the door and Nanette opened it.

Pax led her down the dim corridor. Curiously, she thought she heard Joseph's voice coming down from the nearby staircase. At the base of the steps, Pax pointed at the blanket sticking out of Nanette's pants. Nanette shook her head at him. He mimed putting the blanket over his eyes. And she shook her head at him. Pax crossed his arms and sat on the bottom step.

Nanette huffed and then draped the blanket over her noggin. She let it hang far enough back on her head so she could still see. Pax smiled and began going up the stairs on all fours.

She didn't know why exactly, but her trust in the toddler was dubious at best.

Pax stopped at the top of the stairs.

"You need to know something," he said.

"What?" Nanette was getting antsy.

"Bunk beds are awesome."

"Keep moving, little one."

The pair emerged in the den. Under a standing lamp in the corner sat Roux reading. She dropped her book onto the hardwood floor and sat up. The armchair she sat in was made for someone much larger than her but her widened eyes seemed to fill the whole corner of the room. In a fury, Nanette turned to the toddler. She knelt to his level and pointed a finger at his chest.

"You sold me out!" she spat.

"Roux, it's past bedtime," he said, a little distraught.

Roux didn't know how to communicate to Pax that her bedtime was much later than his without him feeling affronted in some manner.

Nanette thought that she must have been going loopy because she now thought she could hear both Joey and Rich in the next room.

"We can trust her," Pax decided.

"I cannot even trust you. Which way's the kitchen?"

"Through that door."

Roux scampered across the room and grabbed onto the back of her suit. Nanette paused. She waved both of the kids away.

"What?" she said to Roux. "Something important?"

Roux, who didn't care for Nanette's tone, just shrugged her off. Nanette had a lot of respect for the child for just letting her be. Roux understood that she had her own problems. She took Pax by the hand and stepped to the side. Nanette stretched out her shoulders and, proud in her tactful manipulation of the children, pushed through the kitchen door.

On the other side, she saw four grownups. There were two people she assumed were the Fieldings with their backs turned towards her. But the other two were familiar visages facing her.

Rich almost dropped his glass. And Joey took a step back.

Nanette saw the other two adults about to turn around so she ducked back out of the room. Pitying her, Roux grabbed Nanette by the hand and led her across the room. She hid her behind the armchair she was reading in just as Mister and Doctor Fielding came into the den.

"Pax?" said the father. "How did you get out of bed, buddy?"

Nanette felt her chest thumping. This was where it ended, betrayed by an illiterate whelp.

"I'm a spy!" he chirped. There was a hint of nervousness in his testimony.

"I'm sure, Pax," there were the ruminations of the kid being lifted, "but bedtime means bedtime, okay? Playtime is for tomorrow."

"Okay…"

Nanette listened to the descending footsteps of Mister Fielding. She clutched the blue blanket in her hands, strangling it. He didn't sell her out—even when the pressure was on. Resigned himself back to that life behind bars just for the success of the mission. She wrung the blanket in her hands, mourning the loss of a good soldier. Nanette inhaled deeply, but didn't move.

Another person came through from the kitchen.

It was the mother, Nanette discerned as she heard speech.

"Roux, it's time you got ready for bed yourself, yeah? ... Good girl, turn out that light."

Roux appeared beside Nanette. The girl, in the instant she had to look at Nanette before she turned off the standing light, winked.

When the light went out, Nanette listened to two sets of footsteps fading down a hall.

The beating of her chest filled the room as she bided for her moment to rise. The mother had taken the girl. The father had taken the boy. It was too perfect. She got in formation to slink out into the shadows when yet another set of footsteps entered the mix.

"Come out, Nanette."

It was Richard.

"Hush," Nanette instructed, "lest we sacrifice my position at this critical juncture."

"How'd you find us?"

"Skill."

"Joey doesn't want to talk to you."

"Well, alright."

"How did you know we were here?"

"Oh please. Do not think to flatter yourselves, Richard. I am not here to smooth over a petty tantrum."

"Petty tantrum? Jesus Christ, Nanette, you don't even get it, do you? You ruined him. You are a conceited sociopath with no regard to the consequences of your actions because you truly believe that you can do no wrong."

"And what is the problem here?"

"Oh my god. You are."

"Pish. I gave you and Joseph a home when no one else would."

"We wouldn't have needed a home if it wasn't for your big mouth!"

"Debatable. You speak as if you both were not facing particular inevitabilities."

"You're disgusting, Nanette."

"I shower every day."

"You are so dense. Why would you even tell his parents? Huh? What could you possibly have had to gain?"

Nanette said nothing.

"Tell me!"

"There is no reason, Richard. I only had things to lose if you think about it."

"Why would you even come if it wasn't to apologize?"

"What would I ever apologize for? I would rather never appear so weak, so low. If, if—I would say that I had done Joseph a service. Now if you would care to desist in slowing me down, I have to complete my mission."

"Your mission—?! Oh my god, of course. You're not even here for us. You're here for your stupid lunchbox!"

"Stupid?"

"Get out. Get out of this house right now."

"Not until I know if the lunchbox is here or not—"

"Of course it isn't here! We've been in that kitchen all afternoon! It isn't here and it isn't anywhere. That lunchbox was obviously the smartest inanimate object in the world if it could figure out that it wanted to get away from you. Imagine being so insufferable that even your possessions had enough. It's time you go, Nanette. You need to do like your lunchbox had finally done and what Joey and I have put off for way too long. You need to leave."

Nanette swallowed.

She took one step and stopped.

Then she said, "Lunchboxes cannot think for themse—"

"Go."

And Nanette, scurrying like a weasel, hurried by Rich and out the front door into the warm summer night. Rich stood alone in the Fieldings' den as Joey entered the room, though he remained wordless. Callie Fielding then came back from down the hall. She cleared her throat and asked, "Is she gone?"

CHAPTER FOURTEEN

THE TENTH CHILD

Joey and Rich had a fitful night. Set aside the difficulty they had of getting comfortable on Al and Callie's pullout couch with its bar under the mattress digging into their backs, the general unrest of Nanette's persistence to break into homes was enough to madden a lesser man.

Joey adjusted to the darkness, making peace with the insomnia, and took to counting the tiles on the ceiling. Rich tried to wrap his arms around Joey's chest but just couldn't get the configuration right. After a while, he resigned himself to laying his head on Joey's stomach while his feet draped over the edge of the bed.

"She's not finished yet, is she?" Joey mourned.

"She doesn't have the lunchbox, so no. Probably not."

"She's going to get herself arrested."

"It's amazing she hasn't already. She must've been at this for the better part of the past two weeks. You'd have to wonder which houses she hasn't hit yet."

Joey chuckled, but it has a somber intonation, "Yeah." They didn't speak for a few more minutes until Joey resumed, "Suppose she has some houses left. Do you know which they'd be?"

"Well, I was around for Javy, the twins, and Jon. So that's four of the kids."

"And I was there for Meadow."

"And we were both here for the Fielding kids. Which would leave three left."

"No, probably not three. Figgy was one of the first kids making up rules of games that involved Nanette, remember? She must've seen Nanette prowling around her apartment early on."

"Then what about Yuki?"

"I don't know, maybe."

"I don't think so—Yuki had been approaching Javy, if you think about it. If the seven-year-olds were making up games about Nanette, what interest would that have been to Yuki if she only played with the Fieldings who weren't hit until tonight? So that'd bring us up to nine kids."

"Yeah, but that would mean—"

"Oh, no."

"—she's going to die."

Dorie Eliot was the most in touch with the times. She was young, patient, crippled with anxiety, and sharp as a knife. Her biggest problem was her complete lack of power. Everything was about power in her household and her father's obsessive belief that he had none, even though he was the driving force of the whole extended family. Dorie couldn't keep in touch with her brother Rich, not out of disdain for his lifestyle, but because she was not capable of supporting him without her being thrown out of the home as well.

Something as simple as loving her brother would mean that she would need to find a new apartment, a better job than the ice cream stand she scooped at part-time, and there would be almost no way for her to pay for her college outside of scholarships. And even then, Dorie recognized, she was a good student, but she had never been a great student. She never had faced the pressure of needing to be the best. She only had to live up to her family's standards, which unto themselves were a little unwarranted. But Dorie seemed to be the only one who understood her brother. And in doing so, she knew that she couldn't possibly understand what he was going through.

So now, she stood off to the side of her ice cream stand, distractedly thumbing through her Instagram. It was the middle of the day, but the sun hid behind the clouds and the breeze dissuaded many potential ice cream customers.

She stared at the round vats filled with candy colors but wouldn't partake. She was still working off the junk she ate at her birthday party and probably would be doing so until July. She didn't want to show up on campus looking like anything else than absolutely stunning. Dorie was always wondering if she was actually as ugly as she believed herself to be. The answer, for anybody other than Dorie Eliot, would be of course she doesn't look as bad as she think she does. It was rather sad that she couldn't surmount her self-esteem, but such was the way of this one.

After her party, she learned that her father had essentially thrown Rich out. Well, had thrown him out again. Dorie loved Rich for that effort he made. To think that her father had the ability to throw guests out of her own birthday, as if ultimately the choice of the company on her special day wasn't even hers to decide. She hadn't the will to overcome her father though. She couldn't sacrifice the way she lived because she loved her brother. And it devoured her.

She wondered if there was anything sneaky in Eliot blood. Because she knew that she was older now, she was more of her own person, regardless of her father's protestations. She could sleep easily having betrayed the trust of Old Mister Eliot if it meant she could reconnect with Rich. It wasn't Rich who had missed her graduation. It wasn't Rich who had missed her playoffs. It wasn't Rich who missed anything. It was their father who had forced him away. And to her pride, Rich still survived. He had a hot boyfriend and a cool job and an ulcer reserved in their father's gut. Dorie wished she could be that well-adjusted rather than go to bed every night fearing that her teeth grinding would finally lock up her jaw for keeps.

Dorie pulled up her contacts to find Rich's name.

She felt like he needed to trust her again. That she would have walked away with him but she just couldn't. She needed to do what Rich would do, and try.

Doug Allaway had to bring Figgy with him to work. It wasn't a problem because Figgy was easily distracted and he wasn't easy with the idea of drug dealers looking after his daughter.

Yuki Green needed a sitter. Her parents had taken to viciously agreeing with one another, causing an issue that every sitter they looked into just didn't provide enough for their little girl. Tsukuru played with the idea of staying home from the dealership and working on translating a manuscript, but Betty wouldn't let him do it alone. They both had to take the day off.

Whatever Javier's sisters had planned, their mother had cancelled. Their brother wasn't going to play by himself and that was that.

Zola and Virginia Dodd were given games to play by their mother in order to occupy them as she frenetically combed through summer programs that would take two five-year-olds with no notice.

Jon Fletcher stayed home. His mother hoped that nine was old enough.

Meadow had a nanny who thought the little girl was too

loud and needy. Still, the nanny took Meadow to the park, where she swung on the equipment by herself, ate her lunch by herself, and played spies by herself.

The morning was so much fun for Roux and Pax Fielding. They had Mister Joey and Mister Rich all to themselves to make them lunch and play games and there didn't even seem to be a garden that the grownups needed to run away to. Mister Joey and Mister Rich even let them watch television for an hour which never happened until really late in the day. It wasn't until their own parents got home that Joey and Rich needed to go for a little bit.

No one could say what the Tenth Child was doing that day. Some speculated that they still went to Baby Badger and sat in the corner for hours, unperturbed. But in the end, it was likely that they just sat in the corner of their own home. It was tough to say.

Rich had told Callie that his lasagna still needed fifteen minutes in the oven as they passed each other coming through the door. It would be ready before he and Joey would be back for the night, so he encouraged the Fieldings to eat it without them. The boys kept the specifics of their flight from the Fieldings; all they could notice was that both Joey and Rich were wearing dark clothes.

Now they drove across town to the hilly outskirts where only the wealthy and reclusive lived. Outside, an orange sky had died and made way for the humid invasion of storm clouds. The forecast had called for heat lighting. They parked at the base of a winding mason driveway. The pink and crimson bricks aligned in the shape of a serpent slithering its way up to a shadowy Victorian home atop the hill. The surrounding lawn was lush only in a few areas, browning and withering as it got closer to the home. There was a single tree on the estate with a hole in the trunk shaped like an unwavering eye. At the edge of the driveway stood a crooked mailbox with a faded address and surname. The only legible script on the box were the letters *H D S.*

If there were cars parked around the estate, Joey couldn't see any. The drive was empty. Joey thought that if nobody was even home then that would make the work easier for Nanette. All anybody knew about the Tenth Child's family was that Joey dated their mom in middle school and then she married a man who apparently lived in the shadows. The Tenth Child's mother, Jenny Savoy, was rather delightful. It was everything else that gave the guys pause.

The guys weren't positive that Nanette would even show up tonight. But they were pretty damn sure. If she was able to find out where the Fieldings lived without their help then she would be able to uncover this address as well. Rich called it a sting operation. They were staking out the home, waiting to detain Nanette and bring her home. Joey and Rich couldn't tell why she harped on the matter of her lunchbox with such zeal but it was ending tonight.

It was bright through the clouds, but the streetlights still illuminated.

There was the humble percussion of thunder in the distance.

Rich feared that he and Joey would be mistaken for burglars. After all, two strange men, parked at the end of a driveway that wasn't theirs, dressed in dark clothes, was inclined to turn a couple heads. He tried to ease himself with the observation that the road only had about three or four homes on it, all spread far enough apart so that the neighbors might never have to see one another.

Joey was sitting in the driver's seat and took Rich's hand in his.

"How about an apartment?" Joey asked.

"Huh?"

"We'll get an apartment, with a little planter box in the

window."

"We're going to move?"

"Wouldn't you say it's time?"

"I guess it would be odd going back to Nanette's place indefinitely."

"There's a bed of cool soil hanging from the window—so soft you just want to dig your hand in it, swirl it around. And we'll start with something simple, something cute. Like daisies or something."

"Tomatoes!"

"Yes, those are the cutest. And then we'll find another place to rent for the daycare. Won't it be nice? Getting to leave to go to work instead of have to do it all out of our bedroom? We can maybe even hire that teenager that we always thought about to help us. What if we could get a playground? Wouldn't the kids just love a playground? A jungle gym suspended above some electric blue turf. Maybe there are slides and swings and carousels—I can already see some kid pushing another off of the equipment and we have to take them inside to call their parents! Doesn't that sound nice, Rich?"

"This is a lot coming from you."

"Does that make it any less legitimate? Think of it—we can have a quaint and crappy apartment like we always thought we would. We can support ourselves now. We don't need anybody like my cousin or your father. We can do our own thing."

"Just you and me?"

"Just you and me."

"Oh my gosh, I love this. I really wish we weren't staking out this house like skeptical vigilantes to stop your cousin from breaking in for her lunchbox because it feels like it kind of diminishes the moment."

Joey kissed him. He placed his hand up to the side of Rich's face and pulled him in. They were slow, precise, and sure.

"Holy shit," said Joey, breaking away.

He spied the familiar silhouette of Nanette tiptoeing up

the side of the hill.

Joey fumbled to unbuckle himself from Al Fielding's car. By the time Rich was able to catch up with Joey's thoughts, Joey was already halfway across the drive with the clicking of the brickwork under his shoes. Rich was tailing the two Abbots entirely willing to let them do their own thing. Even though Joey was the coolheaded to Nanette's hotheaded, they were both still stubborn Abbots.

Nanette failed to see Joey encroaching whatsoever. She, as always, dressed in one of her preferred suits. Just because she was doing dirty work didn't mean she had to look like dirty work. A principle that she had to compromise on as Joey barreled right into her.

They were about thirty feet out from the manor when Joey tackled her. They flopped over onto the ground with a discomfiting *thud* that froze Rich in his disgusted observer tracks.

Instantly, as they hit the ground, Nanette and Joey began to tumble down the hill. Joey winced every time one of his broad shoulders rammed into the dirt and Nanette had become preoccupied with keeping the prickly grass blades from slicing up her face. Whatever they were arguing about, Rich couldn't discern it as every other second their words were impeded by a heavy *oof.*

At the bottom of the hill, the two Abbots crashed into a dilapidated toolshed. The black paint on the siding was faded and chipped. The window on the side had lost a couple of its panes and as the bodies hit the side, another fell out. The first instances of heat lightning sparked in the sky, making the heavens glow in patches.

Joey and Nanette were scraping at each other in an unflattering pile in the dirt. Nanette tried to grapple onto Joey's lower abdomen so she could try to flip him aside. Joey was too slippery, and too keen to Nanette's methods. He was stronger, but she was faster, and whoever was the smarter one depended on the instance.

Nanette landed a solid kick to Joey's gut, causing him to

stumble back. The both of them hobbled into a stable footing. Joey went to lunge at her once again but she spoke.

"Wait, wait, wait, Joseph," she said hurriedly, forgetting how the phrase hold your horses actually goes, "consider all of your horses that you could be holding right now. Let us slow down and discuss the matters at hand, yes? Yes."

"We're not discussing things, Nanette," Joey stated. "You're coming with me and Rich. We'll drop you off at your house and you'll put all this lunchbox insanity behind you. Okay?"

"What? No, that's a ludicrous proposition, Joseph. In your misguided attempts to restrain me, have you not figured it out? This is the last house. It is the end of the line! The lunchbox has to be in there. It is in there—if all the other houses are clean, and you and Richard never took it, then that leaves one. But one nefarious child to hold the blame for all these past crimes. One child to pay their dues for the strife they have endowed. It ends tonight, Joseph, because this is the end."

"You're not getting in that house."

"Try me, cousin."

"You'll have to get through me and Rich first."

"You and Rich? Please. Where even is he? Hiding and waiting for your cue like he always does? Playing backup?"

"No, he should be..." Joey turned around, expecting to see Rich some distance up the hill. But that wasn't the case—there was no one there. Rich wasn't likely to bail on Joey, especially when he was so passionate about the cause. As Joey turned back to Nanette, he said, "He should be around here—"

Joey didn't finish that sentence either because Nanette was no longer there. And before he could blame her for making a break for it when his back was turned, Joey felt a black bag being pulled over his head.

It took multiple attempts for Joey to get his eyes open.

There was a gross throbbing on the back of his head as if someone played it like a timpani. He gasped as he remembered his mission to stop Nanette from breaking into the Tenth Child's house.

Joey saw that he was fastened onto a steel, armless chair with zip-tie restraints. His hands were tied behind his back and his ankles were secured to the front two legs of the furniture. Joey began to wriggle out of fear.

"Don't bother," said a voice. Joey turned to see Rich tied to another steel chair right next to him.

"Why not?" Joey asked.

Rich gestured with his chin at Nanette currently wriggling on the floor with her chair tipped over.

"I have almost got it," Nanette grunted, obviously being nowhere close to success. She then yelled out something about being Detective Annette G. Store and that whoever lived here was under arrest.

"Where are we?" Joey asked.

"I think it was some sort of dining room," Rich said.

And he was probably right. The room had little in it except for a cabinet on the far wall. There was a massive oriental rug laid over the dark hardwood floor. In the center of the ceiling there hung a copper chandelier with a slight pendulous movement to it. Other than that, the trio couldn't see much else. The chandelier only had a faint glow to it that lit up an unimpressive circle of vision.

"We're inside the house," Joey speculated.

"Oh thank goodness Sherlock finally woke up," Nanette sneered from the floor. "What ever would we do without such brilliant deductions?"

"Shut up, Nanette," Rich said. "We could be anywhere. You were knocked out longer than me."

"I was playing knocked out to see if the assailant would reveal any useful information."

"For fifteen minutes?"

"I will not apologize for dedication, Richard."

"You won't apologize for anything," Joey said, half-interested.

"That's right," she agreed. "We would not even be captured if Joseph had not slowed me down."

"You would've been captured either way, Nanette," Joey offered.

"*Au contraire*," she said, stumbling on the pronunciation. Joey looked away. He was done with her.

The trio heard thunder overhead, and some light rain. It was hard to tell if they were close to a window because they couldn't see lightning or any other luminosity. Joey felt that one of the rods in the back of his chair had a much sharper edge than the other ones, as if the chair was dropped or attacked in that one spot. Quietly, Joey started wearing away at his plastic restraints against the back his chair.

"In fact," Rich said, "if you had just bought a new lunchbox like a normal person, we wouldn't be in this bind at all."

"Normal people are weak and without constitution," Nanette griped.

"What was so special about that lunchbox?"

"Nothing in particular, it just happened to be my lunchbox."

"Are you kidding me?"

"What would you want me to say, Richard? 'Oh, I need that lunchbox back because it was the first gift I had ever received from my darling dearest Grandmother before she tragically passed away in a fire tornado. Some said it was hell personally coming to collect her. It is all I have to preserve her memory.' No. It is just my lunchbox. When you have lunchboxes of your own one day then maybe you will understand."

"Shut up," Joey said.

"Pardon?"

"Shut. Up. Shut up about Grandmother. She's never done anything but love us when nobody else did and you still treat her like hellspawn."

"That is because she needs to know everything about her

family. She needs the control. She is nowhere near the triumph of humanity you may consider her to be, Joseph. You know, she knew about my secret. She knew that I told your parents about your, well, desires. And she sat back and let it consume me for two years. Two years she kept that from you. Your parents did not tell you where they got the information, they did not tell anyone, they hoped it was not true. But Grandmother was so much more astute than to accept the disowning at face value. She discovered it was me because I was the only one who did not care. I was the only one who accepted you. And this, Joseph, this is my recompense."

"Oh, boo-*hoo*, Nanette. God forbid someone holds you accountable for your actions. And you know what? Next time I see Grandmother, I'm going to thank her—thank her for being your demons, for being your jury, because you think you can do no wrong. I didn't tell my parents about me because I knew that they weren't ready. And I knew that I wasn't ready. It was my right to tell anyone—not yours. Because it doesn't, nor did it ever, affect you, Nanette. You didn't save me. You set me up. After those couple months I stayed with you, I was ready to leave but couldn't. Because the second I was about to go— oops, my parents are disgusted with me and can't stand to see me. If you ask me, Nanette, you didn't help me. You helped yourself, like you only ever do, because I think at the end of all your insults you're afraid of being alone again and finally you had a prisoner who could fix that for you. You can talk yourself out of a lot of things, but you can never talk yourself out of loneliness."

The soft tapping of rain gave the room sound.

Rich made his chair hop, like he was looking for an exit.

"I feel like I should give you two a minute," he said. "So just know that if I could do that, I would."

"Thanks, Rich."

"Thank you, Richard."

After the brief exchange of gratitude, Joey managed to snap off the restraints that bound his hands. He cracked his fingers, then massaged his palms to restore a bit of feeling.

A hefty, gravelly voice came out of the shadows then: "Leaving so soon?"

"What?" Joey glanced around, trying to see where the voice came from. "No, not really. I still have to get my feet free, and then I probably would've freed my friends here. We were looking at another fifteen minutes of work. At least."

"Tell me why I shouldn't call the police on you three trespassers?"

"Um, because you've kidnapped us and brought us inside and that doesn't look good either?"

"Joseph, let me talk to him," Nanette said.

"It's not a phone call, Nanette, you can just talk."

"What's she doing on the ground?" the voice asked.

"Saving us," Rich groaned.

"Look," Joey said, "I'm sorry that we were trespassing on your lands. Do you have a child that goes to Baby Badger Cub Club?"

"Why yes," said the voice. "Every day."

"Well, my partner, Rich, and I are the caretakers over at Baby Badger."

"Oh, is everything all right with my child?"

"Yes. You see, my colleague here, Nanette, believes that your child might have taken her—"

"Whooping cough!" Nanette shouted. "You should take them to a doctor with haste. Cough, cough! Cough, cough!"

"Nanette…" Joey trailed off. "Nobody cares about your lunchbox."

Rich added, "You can't just say the word 'cough', Nanette. No one would ever believe that."

The voice exhaled, "Oh, goodness gracious, you're having a laugh. I was worried for a moment there."

"Are you the person who attacked us?" Rich asked.

"I am, apologies," the voice said. "I thought it imperative to protect my home."

"I think we can relate," Joey said.

"If I could ask," said the voice, "why are you here, if it was not to warn me about false diseases?"

"Don't," Nanette barked.

"Nanette lost her lunchbox," Joey said. "She thinks your child might have taken it."

"Are we good?" Rich asked, "Can we be freed from these chairs and talk like normal people? Or will we end up dead by the end of this?"

But no one seemed to hear him.

"A lunchbox you say," said the voice. "I may be so inclined to help you search. But you must do something for me first."

"Do not give him anything, Joseph," Nanette yelped.

"What?" Joey asked the voice.

Two black gloved hands came out of the shadows holding up a deck of playing cards.

"Pick a card," said the voice. "Any card."

"You're... a magician?" Joey asked.

"I need to practice my tricks."

"Oh, god no," Rich groaned. "Please, just kill us."

"Do not give into his dark arts, Joseph!"

"What the hell is going on," Joey murmured as he reached for a card.

"What the hell indeed," said the familiar voice of Jenny Savoy as she flicked on the house lights. When the trio's eyes adjusted they could see that they were in a dining room, just with all the furniture pushed into the corners so they couldn't see it. A tall man in a rose cloak was holding the deck of playing cards. Jenny was holding the hand of the Tenth Child, who seemed nonplussed with the entire situation. The usual perky nature of Jenny Savoy was not present as she scolded her husband, "What have I told you about audience volunteers, Harold?"

"That you can't force someone to be a volunteer," he whimpered.

"That's right. Now release these nice people—Joey? Harold, where did you find these people?"

"Backyard."

"Hi, Jenny," Joey said sheepishly.

"Oh my gods," she said.

The Tenth Child walked over to Nanette and stood her upright, as they did that the Tenth Child whispered two words into Nanette's ear: "Be good." Which was unsettling to Nanette because she was good and because it was probably the only coherent thing either she or the guys ever heard coming out of that child.

Harold left and came back with a pair of scissors and commenced cutting them loose. Jenny spoke for the family, "I don't want to know how you ended up here. I am so sorry. My husband just wants people to help him with his magic but just never knows how to go about it. It's not his usual line of work, you know."

"Is he… a marine?" Rich asked.

"Oh, no," Harold replied, "I code security software."

"Don't bore them with the details, dear," Jenny said. She helped them all up to their feet and asked, "Is there anything we can get you before you go?"

"No—" Joey was cut off.

"Well," Nanette began.

Two minutes later, Nanette, Joey, and Rich were all in Jenny's kitchen. Nanette went back to her practice of checking through all the cabinets. With each cabinet she went through, her search got slower and slower, until she was eventually just standing in the middle of the kitchen with empty hands.

"What's the problem?" Rich asked. But Nanette said nothing.

Instead, Joey spoke for her.

"It isn't here."

Chapter Fifteen

THE LUNCHBOX

It was 5:32 in the morning. Nanette didn't usually sleep in but she thought it was an earned extra two minutes. She pulled herself out of bed, still wearing yesterday's dirt covered suit. There were grass stains all up the arms and there were rips in the material at the elbows and knees. She dragged herself into her home office and looked at the printout version of her spreadsheet hung up on the wall. There was only one unfilled box—the culprit. But as it turned out, none of the children were the thieves she thought them destined to be. Nanette wondered if there was any point to existence.

She ripped it from the wall, bunched it up and threw it out. She stamped it down into her minuscule wastebasket. Then she opened up her laptop and wrote an email she never thought she would: Nanette will not be coming to work today because she has died. Expect her back before the end of the week.

The storm from last night had blown over. Though, that fact was debatable for Nanette. But on the literal scale, the storm was over and she could see the light of the summer sun poking into her house. If she was motivated to do so, Nanette was prepared to shut the blinds on every pane in the house.

But instead, she went into the kitchen with the intention of preparing some breakfast.

She opened up the refrigerator and saw the space where she usually kept her lunchbox, completely void. She couldn't just accept how it was possible that one day a lunchbox just simply stopped being. It was time she faced the truth: she lost her lunchbox. There weren't any children left to blame. Nor were there the guys to blame, she almost made sure of that. Nanette occasionally thought she could hear their voices come up from downstairs, but no. That wouldn't be the case anymore, she had to figure.

Twenty minutes passed with her staring into the fridge.

Nanette enjoyed the cold. Winter was the best month, really. Shame it was summer after all.

The absence of the lunchbox burned her, though. It was as if another childhood was passing. One without such securities that she had relied on for the past few years. Her confidence, her belief in the guys' return to her house had begun to falter. They had always come back. Always. But now it seemed that life no longer afforded certain inevitabilities. Maybe her actions did have consequences, maybe it was true that the occurrences of the past held weight in the future. In which case, oh goodness, what has she done? A lifetime of superiority spent and only now did she realize that those around her might not have recognized that superiority.

She didn't have much planned for the rest of the day. She didn't even know if she was sure about which weekday it was. All she knew was that she had lost. It was a brand-new era.

This was her first failure.

Joey was by himself for the first one, only because Rich had an appointment at noon that he wouldn't miss for the world.

Doctor Fielding let him borrow her car. The apartment was still in town, close to downtown, which might actually give Joey and Rich an excuse to go out every once in a while. Joey kept his hand in his pocket. The storm yesterday made the air cool. Plus, the little velvet box felt too nice not to play with.

The apartment was clean. There was a modest living area that could comfortably house a television and a loveseat. There was also space for a desk so they could finally get their business out of their bedroom. The kitchen didn't have a lot of elbow room, but it was only for two people so it would probably not be an issue at all. Joey was most worried about the microscopic size of the bathroom sink and mirror which would be fine for him if Rich didn't take ages in the morning. Say what you would about Nanette's house, having three bathrooms for three people was nothing short of a blessing.

He walked around the space, turning on and off the faucets, making sure the refrigerator light worked. The bed was larger than the one they shared back at Nanette's which either seemed extravagant or excessive, Joey had yet to decide.

The closet itself in the bedroom was large enough, but it wasn't a walk-in. Joey thought that that was for the best. They didn't need the walk-in anymore and with use of a closet, they could probably get rid of a couple clothes racks, or maybe one of their wardrobes.

All this time, Joey had an eager agent alongside him trying to convince him on taking the apartment. Joey knew he wouldn't probably pick out a place today. And he definitely wouldn't make the call by himself. But still, he sat on the bed to feel how he sank into it. He ran his hand across the carpet to see that it was fluffy and not worn away like at Nanette's. He counted the outlets, asked about hot water, and needed to know how much it would cost to do a load of laundry.

Joey believed that they could do it. He tried to picture Rich being confident singing in the shower with neighbors so much closer by. He wondered what it would smell like without drowning the air with conflicting scented candles. He wondered when they would finally get a car or if Lyft would support them when they finally couldn't borrow from the Fieldings any longer.

In all the wondering, Joey found himself at the window in the living room. He pushed it open to see a tiny, dried up planter hanging from the window.

Joey asked, "Would we be able to put in a bigger box out here?"

"I don't know, I'd have to check. I'm not sure that you could though."

Joey gripped the velvet box in his pocket.

"I don't know," he said, "we'll have to think about it."

Rich didn't know what it was about frozen yogurt that attracted his sister so much, but when he entered the store there she was at the counter with probably the smallest size someone could order. It was the middle of the day so business was fairly sleepy. The shop's bright orange theme almost hurt Rich's eyes but he got over it when Dorie threw her arms around him.

He got a small cup of frozen yogurt. It was birthday cake flavored and he only got a little because he didn't want to overdo anything. But when he saw the buffet of toppings, something inside of him succumbed. He didn't worry if the flavors would conflict when he covered it with maraschino cherries, chocolate-covered pretzels, and coconut shavings. There were actual bits of birthday cake available, and he still threw them in on his yogurt. At the end of the line, he drowned it all in melted caramel and hoped that the regrets would wait to filter in later on that night.

Dorie chose a table outside, even though it was a bit breezy. She sat in the sun with gigantic sunglasses protecting her. Rich, without the foresight to bring glasses, hid in the shade of the umbrella sticking out of the middle of the table. Dorie traded between looking at Rich and looking to the parking lot.

"Waiting for someone?" Rich asked.

"No," Dorie said, smiling, "I wanted to thank you."

"You're welcome."

"You don't even know what it's for!"

"And I probably don't care."

"Well, I wanted to thank you for putting up with me."

"Of course I would. Why wouldn't I?"

"Because, you know, the family." She dramatized the word for him. "And because you know that Pa's never going to change."

Rich mixed his yogurt until it became soupier. "I know."

"But you still try."

"I'm not wasting my time with the family anymore, Dor. I can handle myself."

"Yeah but, like, you know. The Eliot name—I used to think it meant something. And I guess it does. Just not to me."

Rich chuckled. "It's good to see you."

Dorie reached across the table to cup Rich's hands in hers. "I'm sorry for everything."

"You didn't have a choice."

"Of course I had a choice. We all left you. I let that happen."

"Not on your own."

"Well, I'm still sorry."

They picked at their yogurt, catching up about what's been going on since the birthday party—or rather catching up on the past two years because Rich wasn't quite in the mood to talk about what had been going on in his life for the past two weeks.

Dorie looked back to the parking lot and said, "I'm also sorry for this."

And then stepping up to their little table, Rich saw his brother, Cass Eliot, standing awkwardly in a polo shirt and a pair of khaki cargo shorts. The brothers just looked at each other for a minute until Dorie yelled at Cass to sit down.

"Come to your senses, yet?" Cass asked. Dorie tensed her shoulders.

"What?" Rich moved back.

"Your senses. Remember a couple years ago I asked if you were ever gonna be a Bruins fan? And you said you probably already are? And I said you'd come around?"

"Christ, Cass, I was still in college then."

"Well, have you come to your senses?"

Rich grinned, "Oh yeah. Bruins are hockey, right?"

"You're screwin' with me."

"Of course I'm screwing with you. You think I'd admit to not being a Bruins fan in Massachusetts? It's the establishment of hockey itself that I don't give two shits for."

"Hah, yeah." Cass tapped his fingers against the tabletop. He craned his neck as if there were some above-average-sized words struggling to come out. "Look, Rich, about Pa—"

"Pa's a lost cause, Cass, I know that."

"I know you know that, Rich. I didn't think I knew that. I'm sorry for getting you thrown out of the party, I thought Pa would miss you. I don't know—I'd miss my kids even if they were, you know."

"It's not embarrassing, Cass. There's a guy in my life."

Cass sat up in his spot, tapping his fingers faster.

"No, yeah. I know. Look, I'm not gonna pretend that I know what it's like bein' you. There's just some people you can't understand."

"You're telling me."

"I'm just sayin' Pa doesn't control us like he used to. We're our own people."

Dorie chimed in, "You don't have the family, I think Cass is trying to say, but you have us."

Rich looked to his older brother. "That true?"

"It's true."

Dorie squealed. "Look at us! The band's back together."

They spent the rest of their time explaining things to each other. Cass and Dorie tried to explain to Rich how to play football. Rich and Dorie tried to explain to Cass the charms of musical theatre. And Cass and Rich tried to explain to Dorie the necessities of starting up a business.

It wasn't the way things used to be. That much was sure. But it was the way that things were now and the Eliot siblings were learning how to deal with that. Rich made a joke about how the first real conversation he'd had with Cass in years was still about sports but Rich really was the only one to have found it funny. They made plans to meet again, but next time at a place where Cass actually wanted to order something and wouldn't put Rich in a diabetic coma.

After a couple hours, Joey had pulled up to the sidewalk in the Fieldings' car.

The Eliots all bid each other goodbye as Rich pulled on his jacket. He felt around his pocket to make sure that a certain velvet box was still in there. He wouldn't wait forever for Joey to step up, he knew how much that boy enjoyed waiting.

Before Rich got far, Dorie asked, "Rich, is that the guy?"

He didn't know exactly what she meant. Dorie had met Joey during his college years. But all Rich really had to say was, "Yeah, yeah that's the guy."

Joey and Rich, passing by the turtle crossing the road, pulled into the driveway. They wanted to collect a few more things to bring back to the Fieldings' place before Nanette got home. The equanimity of the house bordered on eerie. There used to always be some string of rumors coming through the walls. But not today. They supposed enlivening the house was part of the work they did there.

It was sad how Nanette feared being alone.

Joey and Rich went in through the front door. There was a chill coming down the stairs that piqued the guys' curiosities. The followed the draft up and into the kitchen where they found the refrigerator door wide open. Rich tried to shut it.

"Ouch," said Nanette as the door banged into her side.

"Nanette? Jesus Christ! You look possessed," Rich said, worried.

"How long have you been here?" Joey asked.

"What time is it?"

"Almost five thirty."

"Oh. Almost twelve hours."

"Holy shit."

Rich dragged Nanette over to the kitchen table and sat her down. Joey inspected some of the food to see if it had gone bad with the door open all day. When he shut the door, Nanette jumped from her seat.

"You are back!" she exclaimed.

"To gather a couple of things," Rich explained.

"You are not coming back?"

"No," Joey said, but kindly.

"Well then, Joseph, I am going to have to do something I will probably never do again. I am going to admit that my lunchbox is a lost cause."

"Oh?"

"And such events have led me to believe that my outstanding judgment—though far greater than the average person's—is fallible. I would like to apologize for accusing literally every single child in your care, as well as yourselves, for stealing my lunchbox and I would like to apologize for the subsequent collection of felonies that ensued. But I would definitely like to apologize for trapping you here with me for two years even though I would most likely—definitely—do it again. My methods may be somewhat different the second time around though."

"Okay, Nanette," Joey sighed. "We're going to do something we haven't done in a long time."

Joey went in to hug his cousin. She tensed up every muscle in her body until she reminded herself that a hug was generally a sign of good faith. She raised her arms to reciprocate, but not knowing whether or not to squeeze him lower on his body or higher up Nanette resigned herself to patting his back like he was a delicate set of bongos.

"Go clean yourself up, Netty," Rich advised after the hug. She acquiesced, heading off to her private bathroom.

When they were alone, Rich asked, "Are you sure we can leave her like this? We've been gone less than two days and she's already augmented into some apologetic hermit."

"She'll be fine without us. She's spent most of her life without us."

"Suppose she lets us use her house as the daycare until we find a permanent location?"

"She might. We'd have to talk about it with her. It'd be nice commuting into work, even if the commute was to here. Maybe it'd motivate us to buy a car."

"We could carpool with Roux and Pax."

Joey laughed.

And then he stopped.

He reached into his pocket and pulled out the small velvet box and then lowered himself onto one knee.

"Holy shit," Rich said. "You aren't."

"I am," Joey said.

"You're stealing my thunder."

Rich then pulled out his small velvet box and then got down on one knee. They both opened up the boxes displaying the rings in full view.

"Will you—"

"No will you—" Rich cut Joey off.

"Marry—"

"What if we marry each other?"

"Just take the damn ring."

In a huff, the guys took the ring out of the other one's box and put them on. Joey didn't know if the moment was perfect or not, but decided to accept it as part of who they were.

The doorbell buzzed then. Joey didn't know who it could've been. Nanette didn't have any visitors, generally, and all the parents knew that the daycare was closed for the day due to the definition of unforeseen circumstances.

It was Grandmother. She stood next to a tall suitcase. In one hand she held a plastic sandwich bag but Rich couldn't tell what was inside it.

"Hello, Joey," the old woman beamed.

"Hey, Gran, you want to come in?"

"Yes, but I'm not staying long. Mavis and I are driving back home tonight and we'd like to use as much sunlight as we can. Is Nanette in?"

"Yes, she's just washing up—or getting changed—I don't exactly know."

"She's shedding her skin," Rich called down the stairs.

Grandmother inspected Joey. She saw him in his shoes and in a jacket, and she didn't hear the pitter-patter of little feet or the delighted squeaks of small voices.

"Are you okay?" Grandmother asked. "It's unlike you to take a day off."

"No, yeah, I'm great," he assured her. "It's just been a hectic couple weeks."

"Oh I'll bet."

"You know, Gran, I asked Nanette why she has such trouble with you. I always wanted to know why she demonizes you so much. She thinks you need to be in control of the family. That's a bit intense, don't you think?"

"Well, yes and no, dear."

"Hmm?"

"I mean, who do you think is in charge of the family? Nanette? Your parents? Your cousin Mo?"

"You're telling me you're in charge of the Abbots?"

"Well, yes. Do you remember that day back in 2006? The day with all the paper bags?"

"Yeah, grandpa's heart gave out that day from all the excitement."

"But did it?"

Joey was wading through Grandmother's implications.

"You killed Horatio Abbot?" he burst.

"No! No! I simply whispered into his ear that for dinner we'd be having vegan pizza for his birthday dinner and *poof* that was enough for him."

"I can't believe that the thought of vegan pizza would do a man in like that."

"Sweetie, 2006 wasn't ready for the likes of vegan pizza. And I knew that all too well."

"Grandmother." Nanette and Rich appeared at the top of the staircase then.

"Nanette! It's good to see you."

"We are certainly looking at each other in this moment."

"I came to give you this. It looks like a, a sandwich of

some persuasion."

Nanette came down the stairs to the landing. Grandmother handed her a Ziploc bag that contained two pieces of bread that had turned completely teal with mold. But the precision of the diagonal cut was undeniable, and the condiment distribution was exact. Nanette turned the bag to its side and, breathlessly, she said ham and cheese.

"This was my sandwich," Nanette gasped. "How could you have possibly found it?"

"Well," Grandmother said, "Mavis was driving down the road to let me say goodbye to you before we set off for home. I was so sorry that I couldn't help you find your lunchbox. I called a couple days ago to check in and see if you wanted to go shopping for a new one but for whatever reason the line went dead and hasn't worked since. Anyhow—Oh, where was I? … Mavis! So, but as we came down the street, a turtle practically leapt out in front of Mavis's poor Oldsmobile. She's parked in the driveway now. You know that turtle that's been crossing the street for at least a week now? She swerved out of the way and pulled right up onto your driveway. I got out of the car and rushed over to that unfortunate turtle, but when I got there, lying next to it was this sandwich. I know my granddaughter's handiwork when I see it, so I thought I would hop up the steps and present it to you."

"Wait," Joey said, "The sandwich was right next to the turtle?"

In a flash, Nanette Abbot stepped outside of herself, lost in the memory of that turtle. When did it first appear? She had her lunchbox that day, in her hand, she walked through the kitchen half-listening to Rich and Joey plan their day. What did they say? It's about time we found our own place. Yes. Nanette then walked to her car and placed her lunchbox on the roof to get inside and then—

"That's no turtle!" Nanette exploded as she pushed past Grandmother and dashed across her lawn. She ignored the sweetly colored toy trucks that littered the grass. Joey and Rich were in pursuit right behind her as they got closer to the road.

Nanette saw it, and soon Joey and Rich did, too. It wasn't a turtle crossing the road—there never was a stupid turtle in the street. It was obvious as they got close that it was, undeniably, the lunchbox.

Nanette's soul leapt. After all it was still here! She didn't need to learn anything! As she was steps away from lunging into the road, Joey, yelling, "Watch out," tackled her to the ground.

Before she could yell out in disdain, a school bus sped across the street. It was unable to swerve like any other vehicle.

It all happened so slowly, Nanette and Joey and Rich all watched as Nanette's lunchbox was crushed under the force of such an improbable machine.

When it was over, Nanette was on her knees, staring at her totally flat once-lunchbox. Her carrots splintered, her zipper bent. She was frozen in place. There was a hand on her shoulder and she could sense two men standing behind. As she blacked out, the last thing Nanette heard was Joey saying, "Let's go get a new one."

ABOUT THE AUTHOR

Jack Croughwell likes to collect hedgehog knickknacks and wooden robots. Originally from Methuen, Massachusetts, he moved on to receive his Bachelor's in Creative Writing, Theatre, and Italian Studies in 2017. Now he teaches first-year writing at the University of New Hampshire while working on his Master's degree in English Studies. Approach slowly.